THE STRANGE COURTSHIP OF KATHLEEN O'DWYER

THE STRANGE
COURTSHIP OF
KATHLEEN O'DWYER

ROBERT TEMPLE

FIVE STAR
A part of Gale, a Cengage Company

LIBRARY OF CONGRESS CATALOGING-IN-PUBLICATION DATA

Names: Temple, Robert (Robert Mike) author.
Title: The strange courtship of Kathleen O'Dwyer / Robert Temple.
Description: First edition. | [Waterville] : Five Star, a part of Gale, a Cengage Company, 2022. |
Identifiers: LCCN 2022006881 | ISBN 9781432895662 (hardcover)
Subjects: BISAC: FICTION / Action & Adventure | FICTION / Westerns | LCGFT: Western fiction. | Novels.
Classification: LCC PS3620.E4597 S77 2022 | DDC 813/.6—dc23/eng/20220318
LC record available at https://lccn.loc.gov/2022006881

First Edition. First Printing: December 2022
Find us on Facebook—https://www.facebook.com/FiveStarCengage
Visit our website—http://www.gale.cengage.com/fivestar
Contact Five Star Publishing at FiveStar@cengage.com

Printed in Mexico
Print Number: 1   Print Year: 2023

To my wife, Sheila

* * * * *

PART I
THE STAKED PLAINS

* * * * *

CHAPTER 1

The report of a single gunshot startled Kathleen O'Dwyer awake from the wool blanket that served as her mattress. She rolled onto the dusty floorboards of the wagon and sat up. Outside, grunts and curses erupted from the men sleeping beneath other wagons loaded with trade goods for Santa Fe, and Kathleen heard the scrape of steel muzzles on lashed down crates and the clatter of loose equipment as teamsters snatched rifles and shotguns out of wagons. She reached for the sturdy boots she had purchased for the rough journey. Here, she was on the north bank of the Arkansas a couple of days from Upper Crossing near Chouteau's Island—the heart of hostile Indian country—and Kathleen did not have a firearm. What had she been thinking back in St. Louis? Foolish, she thought, downright foolish to accept without question Captain Freepole's assurance that she did not need a gun. The first woman to travel the Santa Fe Trail, indeed. Why had she ever listened to any of Captain Freepole's crazy schemes?

She dragged on her boots and belted a plain brown, ankle-length skirt over her heavy cotton nightgown. She saw nothing of what went on outside the canvas top that enclosed her wagon. Inside the wagon was about the only privacy she had, but now, Kathleen wished she could see whether Indians crept with scalping knives toward her.

She groped for a handhold on top of the driver's seat that formed the front wall of the wagon bed. She intended to peek out the opening in the arched canvas top of the wagon, but at a string of blood curdling cries, she snatched her hands back to her chin. Then she recognized the triumphant cries as Tom Beckenworth's high-pitched tenor and muttered a curse. With pathetic attempts to impress her, the eighteen-year-old boy had pestered her all the way from St. Louis. What danger had the boy gotten them all into now with his mischief?

Summoning her stubborn Irish courage, she gripped the top of the buckboard seat and climbed from beneath the canvas. The night was bright with stars, and a quarter moon turned the gently waving grass of the plains into a silver ocean. The other wagons stood out in stark definition on the flat prairie. Stumbling by her, men rushed toward the sound of Tom Beckenworth's voice. She jumped down and ran after them.

"Miss O'Dwyer, you ain't supposed to be out of the wagon at times like this!"

Kathleen halted and turned to face Captain Freepole, leader of the expedition. A stout man no more than five feet five inches tall, he trotted toward her with his potbelly bouncing up and down, but his back was straight and his shoulders thrown back. The familiarity with which he handled his long rifle and the jut of his chin reminded Kathleen that he had once been an officer in the Kentucky Militia during the War of 1812.

"Get back in the wagon."

"And be murdered alone while all you men run off to who knows where?"

He scowled and ran toward the gathering of men forty yards to the rear of the last wagon. Kathleen picked up her skirt and ran alongside him, her longer stride matching his waddling run.

Tom Beckenworth stood with legs spread well apart, rifle grasped in his left hand and a huge grin on his face. A lock of hair hung down on his forehead. A crumpled shape lay at his feet. Moonlight glinted off the blade of a large skinning knife

Tom pulled from his belt. He crouched on one knee above the crumpled shape of an Indian corpse, grasped the Indian's long black hair, and lifted the dead man's head.

"Good God!" German Joe Holtz bellowed. Holtz was one of three mountain men serving as expedition guides. Holtz's shadow, a half-breed named Billy Gap Tooth, was the second of the guides and stood beside Holtz. Kathleen wondered where the third guide, James Colter, was. Holtz shook his rifle at Tom. "You the greenest little jackdaw of a child ever sucked his Momma's tit. You go lifting the hair of that there Injun, and ya'll might as well dig ya'll's graves come sun up."

"I aim to scalp me this here horse stealing Injun I kilt," Tom said and sawed at the top of the skull. "I don't reckon you'll crow so loud about that scalp string of yourn, not after tonight."

Kathleen clamped her teeth together and watched the grisly sight. Now was no time to betray weakness, not with the way these men treated any trace of weakness. She wished she was back in St. Louis—far better to fend off a hundred widowers like Caleb Jenkins than to deal with this. The knife sliced flesh away from the Indian's skull. He was a short, dark man with legs even more heavily bowed than those of the three mountain men. He resembled a large child with his long, slipper-like moccasins and skimpy leather breechclout. He had no facial hair, not even eyebrows. German Joe spat and resumed cursing.

"You damn fool! You—"

"Mr. Holtz, that's enough cussing," Captain Freepole said. "I've told you before to mind your mouth in front of Miss O'Dwyer.

"Tom, killing a thieving Injun's one thing, but acting like a savage Injun's another. As long as I'm paying the wages on this trip, no man—especially my wife's kin—is going to lift scalps."

"I caught him thieving horses and I kilt him," Tom replied. He was the youngest member of the expedition. Kathleen knew that Captain Freepole looked on Tom as the son his wife had never born him. Someday, the young man would take over the trading firm with Freepole's blessing. "It's for me to do with him as I like, and I say I'm going to lift his hair."

"Boy, you're young, so I'm letting them hot words pass," Freepole said and then gestured with his rifle at Kathleen, "but I can't let this go no further in front of Miss O'Dwyer."

Hands frozen on the Indian's skull, Tom looked at Kathleen. She let none of the horror but all of the loathing for this senseless act show on her face. Tom's eyes wavered.

"Miss O'Dwyer, please go back to the wagons," Tom said. "Captain Freepole's right. A woman hadn't ought to see this."

"Were you planning to show me the scalp later on?" Kathleen asked. Tom's eyes dropped. "Did you think that would impress me?"

"You hear that, boy?" Holtz snorted. "Even the schoolmarm knowed you's wrong. Damn near as smart as she is purty. Boy, let ole German Joe tell you just how wrong you is. Ain't much about Injuns I don't know, and I know for a plumb sure fact this here buck's a Comanche. You kilt him for nothing worse than horse stealing. How many you figure one brave was going to make off with? The whole kit and kaboodle?

"Stealing horses is what every mother's son of a Comanche's born to do. It's their way of collecting toll for crossing their land. But no, ain't bad enough you go kill one. You got to lift his hair to boot. You done fixed this bunch of pilgrims good. We still got halfway to go before we reach Santa Fe. Them Comanches going to make it hell to pay every step of the way. Ya'll be thankful if they leave the hair on nary a one of ya'll.

"And the Missy here you been so sweet on. Did you stop and think what them bastards'd do to her? No sireee! Some buck's going to latch onto—"

"Mr. Holtz, I warned you once already to mind your mouth!"

Captain Freepole shouted. Glaring at the vulgar mountain man, Kathleen brushed back a lock of the flame red hair that fell down her shoulders. Holtz leered at Kathleen. She felt the other men's eyes on her but controlled her reactions, neither blushing nor dropping her eyes. She drew herself up to her full five feet ten inches and stared down at Holtz. More than once, she had intimidated men with her size, but Holtz's leer only broadened.

"Captain, I'm just letting everybody know what's in for them," Holtz said. His eyes squinted, and his lips pulled back from his teeth. "Folks should be obliged to me for telling them straight. I got the smarts some ain't. I'm just doing all concerned a favor. I'm . . ."

While Holtz blustered, Kathleen looked away from the circle of men. Holtz and the half-breed were outcasts. She wondered again where the third mountain man was. James Colter kept to himself. Perhaps, he had left the rest to whatever fate the Comanche intended. Mountain men were a strange breed. They dressed much in the manner of the frontier scouts described by her favorite author, James Fenimore Cooper, but during her two years in St. Louis, she had seen too many vicious brawls among mountain men celebrating the end of trapping season. Natty Bumpo was a common drunk, thief, and back stabber on the streets of St. Louis. Decent people avoided him.

"I ain't seen any other Comanche among the horses or wagons so far," James Colter said. He was suddenly there, not quite at the fringe of the gathering. Startled faces turned in his direction. "Ya'll best break up this church social and keep an eye on the stock yourselves. Bound to be more of them Yamparikas sneaking about."

The other men streamed back toward the double row of wagons while Captain Freepole shouted needless commands to check the wagons and draft animals. With Billy Gap Tooth at his side, German Joe trotted toward camp cursing the greenness of the others. Even Tom Beckenworth raced back, leaving the Indian's scalp hanging by a single flap of skin from the bloody skull. Kathleen turned away from the sight.

"We'd best get back with the rest," Colter said. About twenty-five feet away, he made no move to come any closer, as most of the teamsters would have after speaking to her, and he looked away when she met his eyes. Expression closed and wary, he studied the prairie around him, glanced once more at her, and shifted his gaze again to the prairie. Colter was a misfit, as skittish as the animals he trapped. She murmured agreement and walked toward the wagons. She noticed that he followed, but at a distance.

Back inside the wagon, she took off her boots and socks but not her skirt, despite the stuffy May heat inside the enclosed wagon. She hunted through her belongings and found her hairbrush, but the brush stretched the skin of her scalp tight. She dropped the brush. She picked up a white towel, dipped a corner in a basin of water next to her blankets and wiped her face. Then she wrung out the towel and tossed it on top of the brush. The image of the scalping refused to leave her mind. Most of the teamsters had eagerly watched the mutilation. Holtz's only concern had been Comanche revenge. Colter had hardly glanced at the corpse.

She sat on a stack of packing crates and wondered whether this time she had taken on too large a task. If she had stayed in St. Louis, she could have put off Caleb Jenkins awhile longer—at least until she found a new teaching position closer than Santa Fe, New Mexico. She had dealt with a Caleb Jenkins in every city: Boston, Baltimore, Pittsburgh, and New Orleans. She knew the signs. She had at least six more months before her neighbors stopped finding her obstinate rejection of Caleb Jenkins amusing and questioned why a single woman of twenty-eight spurned the proposal of a respected widower storekeeper. She had perhaps a full year before parents began to keep their children away from her classroom. Until then, she would have had children to sit on the benches she had made out of scrap lumber, children to work arithmetic on the sheet of slate she had framed and hung on the wall, and children to study grammar out of the books she had carried across half a continent. Before St. Louis, she had never run away; she had to be starved out.

But in St. Louis, Caleb Jenkins had a daughter with limp blond hair, narrow hips, and hungry eyes. Sarah Jenkins had endured two years without a teacher when Kathleen reopened the wood frame schoolhouse. One of Jenkins's neighbors had used it for a storage shed for the furs he bought from trappers and Indians. While Kathleen swept out mounds of hair, thirteen-year-old Sarah had come to the door with a basket of food and offered to help. Together, they had scrubbed walls and floor with lye water to remove the stink of animal grease and mildew, dismantled wooden storage shelves and bins, and hammered this lumber back together as benches and desks. Sarah's blue eyes watched while Kathleen explained how much lye to put in a bucket of water or how wide to make the benches. The child used scrub brush and hammer without hesitation. She never missed a spot on the walls or misjudged the height of a bench leg.

When they paused for lunch, the questions poured out of her like water from an overturned jug. Did Miss O'Dwyer teach more than arithmetic and grammar? Sarah had heard of geometry and algebra. Did Miss O'Dwyer teach those? Was there more to reading and writing than just grammar and spelling? Would Miss O'Dwyer teach poetry? Had she ever seen a real play?

The first week of school, Sarah stayed after to help tidy up and asked for harder lessons. Kathleen started her on algebra and French. Soon, Sarah studied Shakespeare. Whenever Kathleen opened the school door in the morning, Sarah perched on the steps helping other girls with their lessons. The older boys wrestled or tossed knives a few feet in front of Sarah. Winners invariably called triumphs to her attention.

As months passed, Kathleen fretted at the way the older boys gathered more and more around Sarah. Her hair was the shade of ripening corn, and her grey eyes the color of grass smoke, but her bones were thin and brittle looking. Her hips were especially narrow. Her veins lay close to the surface of the skin and looked ready to burst at the slightest pressure. People often remarked how much Sarah favored her mother, who had died giving birth to her only child. Kathleen added Spanish to Sarah's after-school instruction.

At the end of Kathleen's ninth month in St. Louis, Caleb Jenkins had come to the schoolhouse late one afternoon and told Sarah to run along home and start supper. Then he turned to Kathleen and asked to speak to her for a moment. He was a tall man, as tall as Kathleen, and looked more like a blacksmith than a dry goods storekeeper. His brown hair was oiled and carefully parted. He wore an ill-fitting black coat, homespun white shirt, and a poorly knotted, black, bow tie. With his arms folded across his chest, he studied Kathleen. His gaze roamed up and down her broad shoulders and hips, her firm arms and legs, her full bosom. There was nothing vulgar or leering in his expression; rather, he studied her as if she were a potential brood mare for his draft horses. His head just barely nodded. She told him to speak his mind.

He said Sarah needed a mother. The girl hardly spoke of anyone else besides Miss O'Dwyer. He saw how good Miss O'Dwyer was with children, especially Sarah. He was a decent Christian, willing to overlook that Miss O'Dwyer was Catholic.

As a prosperous merchant, he could provide for many children. No!

Sarah had stayed away from school for two days. Then she came to class with red, swollen eyes. She fumbled through her lessons. When Kathleen dismissed class for the day, Sarah started for the door behind the other children. At the doorway, she turned and asked whether Kathleen wanted her to stay for Spanish grammar drill.

"What do you want, Sarah?"

"I want you to be my momma."

But Kathleen had turned away and scrubbed the blackboard. Two days later, Captain Freepole had come to her with his silly scheme to ingratiate himself with the Mexican authorities by bringing a good Catholic schoolteacher to Santa Fe. She accepted immediately. She had run away from a small girl about whose future she feared she knew too much; now, she was here among Comanche and other violent men about whose ways she knew very little.

She thought again about guns. She had never touched one. She disliked guns. All the same, back in St. Louis, she had suggested obtaining one but readily accepted Captain Freepole's assurance that there was no need. Perhaps, a gun was one of the tools she must now learn to use.

The head and shoulders of James Colter appeared in silhouette a few yards from the wagon. He glanced into the wagon, met Kathleen's eyes, and looked away. Then he was gone from view, passing on with his survey of the terrain around the wagons. In her need for information, Kathleen decided to gamble on Colter's wary solitude.

"Mr. Colter," she called out, paused a moment, and then called again. "James Colter."

"Ma'am?"

The moonlight highlighted smallpox scars that pitted his

weathered face. His eyes were cold blue, intelligent, and shy with suspicion. He was tall, six feet even, lean and supple like his buckskin clothing. His neck-length brown hair contained no grey; she guessed his age at five years either side of her own.

"I wonder about Mr. Holtz's warning concerning the Comanche?" She picked her words with care, keeping her tone formal and unemotional. His eyes flickered from her face to the surrounding prairie. He shifted his weight from right to left foot, looked back at her and then away again. She suppressed a smile. "I'm sure you will agree that Mr. Holtz talks a great deal about a number of things but not always in the most believable fashion?" He glanced over his shoulder toward the northern horizon. "Don't you agree?"

"German Joe does talk a heap more than he ought to."

"Is he to be believed about these Indians?"

Colter looked straight at Kathleen. "That Injun was a Comanche."

"But was Holtz exaggerating the certainty of attack?"

"He wasn't lying none then. Too scared."

"You just agreed with Mr. Holtz that the dead man was a Comanche, so why did you earlier call him a Yama . . . Yampar . . . Yam . . ."

"Yamparika." At least, Colter spoke without the crude vocabulary that marked German Joe's speech. "Type of Comanche. Could tell by the beadwork on the moccasins. Besides, his eyebrows were gone."

"Why is that?"

"Most Injuns don't like hair on the face. Comanches hate it more than most. Pull it all out, including the eyebrows. Sure sign of a Comanche." He no longer fidgeted from one foot to another, but those cold wary eyes were never still.

"And they will attack?" she asked.

"That boy scalped a Comanche," he said. "That's a powerful

insult to Comanche. If he'd been a Kiowa . . . close friends of the Comanche . . . Kiowa might think twice about jumping so large a group of whites, thirty of us. That won't mean squat to Comanche. They're going to kill at least one of ya'll."

Kathleen looked away. Fear, she had tried to run away from it. Now, here it was again, all around her. Mocking her.

"Funny you calling me 'James.' "

"What?" Kathleen jerked her attention back to the man standing in front of her. With a shock, she realized a hint of longing had crept into Colter's voice.

"Ain't nobody called me 'James' since my ma died. Jim will do just fine, if you want."

"Thank you for answering my questions, Mr. Colter. Goodnight." She sat down on the floor of the wagon, using the raised driver's seat to block him from sight.

CHAPTER 2

The expedition traveled two more days before reaching the ford at Upper Crossing. During that time, they kept the Arkansas River close by on their left for a shield. They saw no sign of Comanche. After the first day passed without Indian reprisal, Captain Freepole and his teamsters drifted along with their heads on their teams, rather than craning their necks from side to side searching the horizon, as the mountain men did.

Holtz and Billy Gap Tooth rode out front of the caravan with backs tense and rifles across elbow crooks. James Colter rode far to the north away from the noise and dust of the wagons. He frequently disappeared into the plains without saying a word to the others, keeping even more to himself.

What the trading party did see were enormous buffalo herds sprawled across flat grasslands. Kathleen had seen small herds in Missouri, but that had not prepared her for the vast numbers that roamed the high plains. Thousands and thousands of buffalo. Often a single herd stretched without break from horizon to horizon. Most times, the great shaggy brutes stood placidly grazing. Then for some unfathomable reason, the creatures went thundering across the prairie making the earth tremble and raising a dust cloud for miles. They were an awesome, thrilling, and somewhat frightening spectacle. Kathleen was aware of seeing the world on a grander scale than ever before in her life, though this made her even more aware of the trading party's isolation.

Kathleen always sat beside Captain Freepole when the expedition moved. His rifle butt stuck over the back of the seat. He wedged the rifle barrel between a crate and the sideboards of the wagon bed for easy grasp. Kathleen glanced at it every now and then, taking comfort from its presence but wishing for one of her own. She observed that a few of the other teamsters owned Kentucky or Pennsylvania long rifles similar to Freepole's, but most contented themselves with shotguns of varying gauges. However, the mountain men possessed rifles of a distinctly different style. She had a couple questions about those guns.

They arrived at Upper Crossing not long before sunset and made camp on the north side of the river. Colter, Holtz, and the half-breed forded the river on horses to scout the far side while the trading party settled down to sleep and rest the draft animals for the morning crossing.

Right after breakfast the next morning, a huge buffalo herd ranged across the plains three to four miles to the immediate north of the campsite. The teamsters busied themselves setting up an anchor line on both sides of the river, rearranging wagon loads, and hitching extra animals to the first few wagons for more pull in the river current. German Joe and Billy sat their horses down by the Arkansas and amused themselves by scoffing at the efforts of the teamsters. A little distance off by himself, James Colter crouched on his heels with horse reins in one hand and a mug of coffee in the other. Kathleen tended a pot of coffee at the cook fire for the teamsters. She sidled across to Colter and extended the pot.

"Your cup need warming?"

He glanced up. Squinting, his eyes shifted between her face and the coffee pot. Good. He waited a second before holding out his cup for a refill.

"I'm curious as to why your and the other guides' firearms

are so different from the rest?"

"Ours are Hawken," Colter replied and looked toward the north. She marveled again how his cold blue eyes were never still but were continually on the move searching, suspecting, discovering. He shifted his weight from his heels to his toes, as if about to stand and move off. She wondered what had made him so distrustful of the company of others.

"Please forgive my ignorance," she said to hold him there just long enough for the information she wanted, "but why are Hawken guns better than, say, Captain Freepole's?"

"Sam and Jacob Hawken make rifles better fit for out here."

"In what way?"

"The barrel and stock's shorter for one. Makes it easier to handle on horseback."

"Is there anything else?"

"Sure." He studied a hawk circling above the northern horizon. "Caliber's a heap bigger—mine's a fifty-four—so what we hit, goes down. That thirty caliber of his is all right for deer and such, but wouldn't even slow up a grizzly or a buffalo."

"How about a man?" she murmured. He glanced at her from under arched brows. His eyes were still. She suppressed an urge to look away.

"Oh, his would kill a man all right, if that old flintlock touched off the powder when he pulled the trigger. I wouldn't trust it in a squeeze. Ball and cap like my Hawken is better. Everything about a Hawken is better. Hawken brothers make them plain and simple but strong as you'd ever need."

Captain Freepole shouted for Kathleen to come sit beside him in the second wagon. She thanked Colter, poured the rest of the coffee on the fire, and walked to the wagon. She reached up and grasped the hand Freepole extended to help her climb in the wagon. Once seated on the buckboard, she glanced back and noticed Colter still crouched on his heels, next to his horse.

He stared a moment in her direction. Then his eyes switched their restless gaze to the open prairie to the north. She worried about that brief stare.

Two men on the far bank hammered a thick post into the ground. Then a third teamster went to clove hitch one end of the rope to it, but he stumbled and let go of the rope. The current pulled that end of the rope into the river. The teamster had to wade into the water to retrieve it while the teamsters holding the other end of the rope hooted at him from the north bank. Once he retrieved the line and wrapped it around the post, the free end on the near side of the river was passed through the harness of the lead animal in the team of the first wagon. Then the men on the near side clove hitched their end to another post. The teamsters on both sides of the river took firm grips on the rope, braced their feet, and leaned back to hold the line taut. The rope would steady the team while it traversed the current.

Colter rode alongside Kathleen and Captain Freepole.

"Captain, that buffalo herd's heading our way." Colter jerked his head toward the north. Freepole and Kathleen turned to look. The slowly moving dark mass raised a considerable dust cloud.

"Yeah, I see." Captain Freepole nodded and turned toward the river. He shouted at his sweating men. "Let's get across sometime today. Get the first wagon rolling."

Despite Freepole's exhortations, the first wagon strained for each foot against the pull of the current. The driver kept the reins tight, pulling the horses' heads out of the water for control. The horses, in turn, could not throw all of their weight into a straight ahead pull but had to lean upstream. Kathleen glanced back. The buffalo eased toward them like a dark smoking ocean tide. Dust obscured the far half of the herd from view. She wondered why Colter was concerned about such a common sight, a herd of buffalo. Captain Freepole and the teamsters ignored the herd. Kathleen leaned back in her seat. The men on the near side unhitched the line from their post.

"Geeyup," Capt. Freepole called to his team and steered the wagon to the river bank. The men passed the line through the harness of the lead horse, secured it to the post, and set their feet to anchor the line. Then Freepole urged his team into the river.

Just then, Holtz and Billy Gap Tooth kicked their horses' flanks and splashed past the wagon. Twice, Billy twisted in the saddle to look back at the buffalo herd. Kathleen looked over her shoulder again. The herd was less than a mile away and coming fast. Colter stood in his stirrups, straining his eyes at the herd. Suddenly, he turned and lashed his horse with the reins.

"STAMPEDE!" Colter shouted. He brought his animal to a splashing, twisting halt beside Kathleen and shouted across her at Freepole. "Get this wagon across. The rest of the wagons will have to run for it."

Then he lashed his horse and rode on. Captain Freepole snapped the reins at his team.

"HEEYAH, YAH, HEYAH!" Freepole cried. Kathleen clung to the sideboards. At the earth's trembling, the teamsters on the north side cried out in alarm and abandoned the guide rope, scrambling for their own wagons. Kathleen and Freepole were barely a third of the way across the river. A swelling thunder muffled the frantic yelling of the men on both sides of the river.

At the sound of thunder, Kathleen twisted on the seat and stared at the north bank. The buffalo herd, except for the first few rows of tossing brown heads, was cloaked by dust that stretched for two miles east to west. The teamsters on the north bank whipped their horses and mules in a desperate attempt to outrace the edges of the herd. She saw most were not going to make it.

The wagon lurched, jerking Kathleen's head around. The team had spooked at the sound of the oncoming stampede. Without the guide rope to hold them steady, the horses kicked and thrashed against each other. Freepole fought to hold the team straight for the opposite bank. If the horses slewed around to left or right, the wagon would upset.

Kathleen hung onto the sideboards. She was amazed to see Colter sitting his horse two thirds of the way across the water calmly watching the scene. He made no move to come to their assistance, as did several of the teamsters on the south bank, who waded out into the current to grab the horses' harness and to lead them ashore. Ignoring the wagon, Colter watched the oncoming buffalo.

Forced on by the weight of their brethren running full tilt behind them, shaggy behemoths plunged into the water for fifteen yards before slowing. The foremost beast finally stopped neck deep in the water while thunder droned along the river banks to east and west. The entire north side of the Arkansas swarmed with angry, plunging, snorting buffalo.

The wagon climbed out of the water and up the south bank onto the dry prairie flat land. Captain Freepole halted the team parallel to the river not far from James Colter. The teamsters lucky enough to be on this side of the river crowded alongside their leader's wagon, all cursing and shouting at once. Each gestured at the far bank and demanded to know what to do next. Captain Freepole slumped against Kathleen and sobbed, "Tom, Tommy boy."

Billy Gap Tooth snickered. Kathleen glowered at the half-breed while she cradled the captain's head against her shoulder. German Joe slapped Billy on the knee, pointed at Kathleen, and grinned. The half-breed returned the grin. In disgust, Kathleen looked away. Colter, where he sat his horse and studied the north bank, caught her eye.

"Is there any hope for those on the other side?" she asked. He shook his head. "Surely Tom and some of the men were able to outrun the stampede? Maybe they need our help to cross the river farther down?"

Colter infuriated her. He did not seem to find the slaughter of his companions the source of humor that Holtz and the half-breed did, but his calm, unreadable expression displayed not even that much entanglement with the dead men.

"They didn't outrun the Comanche," Colter said.

"What do you mean? What Comanche?"

"Those who stampeded them buffalo," Colter replied. "Ain't natural for them critters to move all that way toward us without stopping to graze, then stampede just when we was crossing the river and too close to get away. They was driven. The sort of trick Comanche love."

"Yes sirreee!" Holtz cried. "I warned ya'll dang fools about them Comanche. Told ya'll what to expect, but would anybody listen to ole German Joe? No sirreee, kept right on like we was out for a Sunday stroll. Now look at the fix ya'll's in. Now, maybe ya'll listen to old German Joe."

CHAPTER 3

To Kathleen's dismay, the disaster at Upper Crossing broke Captain Freepole. The straight-backed little gamecock of a trader, bent on cornering the American market to Santa Fe, became a hunch-shouldered, pot-bellied, old man bowed down by grief, troubling himself only with tending the team of his own wagon. Two of the five surviving teamsters had lost their guns at the Arkansas fording. Their eyes were wide and staring, their hands twitchy. The other three men clutched their firearms with both hands, their eyes shifting from Captain Freepole to the three scouts. German Joe Holtz and Billy Gap Tooth looked at each other and grinned. "Me and Billy, here, crossed these plains a heap of times," Holtz crowed. "We know what needs doing and how to do it. Ya'll just pay attention to what we say, and this here bunch of pilgrims will get home safe."

The five teamsters exchanged stares and nodded. Then one said, "We hear you, Joe."

Kathleen's contempt was tempered by her own sense of weakness without a gun. She tried to catch Colter's eye, but without so much as a glance at anyone, he touched heels to his mount and rode west at a trot. Laughing and cursing at the others to come on, Holtz and Billy set out after Colter. The teamsters scrambled into their wagons and whipped up their teams. Kathleen climbed up beside Captain Freepole, who sighed and flicked the reins to his mules. Kathleen knew that among the cooking utensils in the wagon was a short, stubby butcher knife that would tuck into the waistband of her skirt. Not a rifle, but well, something. She had never felt this weak, and she cursed her blind arrogance that had led her into this catastrophe.

The two wagons stayed close to the Arkansas River, as they continued west, but the Arkansas was a mineral polluted river. The wagon carrying the extra water kegs for the draft animals had been lost at Upper Crossing, so they had to ration their drinking water. Each wagon had a water barrel the travelers had to replenish from unpolluted springs and brooks, but these were few and far between. The mountain men knew where to search for them, but Holtz and Billy Gap Tooth stayed with the main body, leaving Colter the dangerous task of scouting for water alone. Each dawn, he wolfed down a bite or two of corn pone and salt pork Kathleen fried over the fire, drank a swallow of her coffee, and then rode off while the other men lingered over their morning smokes. He often disappeared for most of the day. Each morning, Kathleen half expected him to strike out on his own, leaving the others to whatever fate awaited them, but he always returned and led them to clean water.

On the fifth day after the stampede, the two wagons stopped to refill water casks beside a small stream that Colter had discovered. Kathleen told Captain Freepole to excuse her for a few minutes. He nodded.

"Where you off to now, Missy?" Holtz sat his horse while the teamsters filled the water casks. As usual, Billy Gap Tooth sat his horse next to Holtz.

"I have to attend to a private matter," Kathleen said and pointed toward a screening stand of mesquite a hundred yards away.

"Whoa, hold on there." Holtz grinned. "We can't be standing on manners and such anymore, not least ways while them Comanche no doubt dogging our trail. Ain't that right, Billy?"

The half-breed nodded and showed the reason for his name in a broad grin. The teamsters slowed work to watch—a couple of them smiled. Colter stood by his horse where it slaked water from the stream, watching the prairie horizon well to the south of the water hole. Kathleen glanced at Captain Freepole, who sat on the wagon seat and stared at the backs of his team.

"I said this was a private matter." She kept her voice steady, matter of fact, and met Holtz's leer without flinching. The way things stood with the expedition, she wanted to avoid a quarrel, if possible.

"Me and Billy better go with you then." Holtz winked at his shadow, Billy Gap Tooth, who nodded his head. "Wouldn't want them Comanche coming along and lifting your hair while you're all alone."

"I do not need your protection," Kathleen said and then raised her voice. "Captain Freepole."

The merchant lifted his gaze from the backs of his team and wiped a hand across his brow. He sighed.

"Let her be, Holtz," Freepole said. "It don't look to me like she's in any danger just the other side of that stand of brush."

"Well, there's some as say you don't know a heap about them dangers." Holtz spat a stream of tobacco juice whose tail end dribbled down his beard. He looked at the motionless teamsters, but the men eyed one another without making a move. Holtz's grin broadened.

"I say it's dang foolishness for this woman," Holtz said, "to go traipsing off by herself. If she's bound and determined, well, somebody's got to watch out for her."

"Captain Freepole, I insist." Kathleen stared at the merchant. He looked away, but she waited for his eyes to meet hers again.

"She goes by herself." Freepole picked at a fret on his shirtsleeve.

"Says who?" Holtz responded. Billy Gap Tooth had lost his

grin. He studied Captain Freepole, glanced at Holtz out of the corners of his eyes, and then looked back at Freepole. Holtz still smiled, but it was a tight-lipped expression. Paying no attention to Kathleen, he glanced around the assembly of men, looking last at Colter, who stood beside his horse, rifle in the crook of his left arm, right hand scratching his neck as if nothing of any importance was happening. But his eyes watched Holtz.

"I SAY!" Captain Freepole roared and made half a motion to seize his rifle from behind the seat. Holtz and Billy rested thumbs on the hammers of their rifles. "I'm paying the wages on this trip, and what I say still goes. You hear me, Holtz?"

"Oh, I hears you. And I'm thinking them wages ain't amounting to much next to losing my hair." Holtz cast a quick glance at Colter. "How you reckon, Colter?"

"I reckon it ain't no concern of mine, if she wants to lose her hair going off by herself. It's her hair," Colter said. Holtz studied the other mountain man a moment longer.

"I reckon that makes sense," Holtz said and smiled. The stiffness eased out of him and Billy Gap Tooth. Their thumbs drifted from rifle hammers.

"Well, go on then, Missy." Holtz waved his hand at Kathleen. "Go get your high falooting business done with."

On her way to the mesquite stand, Kathleen tried to walk without showing the tremble in her legs. She was safe, she thought, for now. But how long could she trust Freepole's sagging authority and Colter's obscure intentions? Better to trust her own wits; yes, better to think her way around the next incident, and the next, but it was a long journey to Santa Fe.

The next day, late in the afternoon, Colter galloped back to the main party from a scout to the south. The other two mountain men reined in their horses to wait for him. The two wagons took their cue from Holtz and halted, too. Colter pulled up his horse and gestured to the southeast.

"Comanche."

"That their dust?" Holtz jerked his head toward the southeast. Colter nodded.

"How many?" Holtz asked.

"Fifteen or sixteen, near as I could tell."

Holtz twisted in his saddle and bellowed at Captain Freepole and Kathleen. "Guess we'd better be getting on then."

One of the teamsters, a lanky, sandy-haired man named George Croftin, held his floppy-brimmed hat like a man asking a priest for absolution. George had lost his shotgun at the Arkansas fording. "Joe, you think we can outrun them?"

"Nah, they're Comanche," Holtz said. "Best we can do is find the wagons a better place to fort up. No cover here, except the wagons. They might make do, but I ain't eager to try it."

With Holtz and Billy Gap Tooth thirty yards in the lead, the expedition traveled at a brisk trot. Colter rode to the rear and a little to one side of the wagon with Kathleen, Freepole, and George Croftin. Although they had Captain Freepole's old flintlock in the wagon, Kathleen was glad Colter was close at hand. He had a rifle, but she wondered how much reliance to place on him. She had no doubt the mountain man knew he was safer on his own.

The dust cloud to the southeast grew larger. After a while, Kathleen was able to make out the Indians beneath it. Sunlight reflected off their copper flesh and the horns of buffalo skulls many wore as helmets. Weaving a fiery spotted pony back and forth across the prairie at breakneck speed, each Comanche tried to outdo his companions with daring displays of horsemanship—swinging down to one side and snatching clumps of grass, swinging beneath the belly of his horse and up the other side, and tossing a lance in a high arc out ahead and then racing to catch it before it fell to earth. All the while, the Indians barked gleeful war cries and long, ululating yells. They closed to within two hundred yards of the last wagon, cavorting like performers in a circus. Colter rode up beside her wagon.

"Why don't they attack?" Kathleen shouted.

"They're letting us get good and scared by the sight of them first," he shouted back. "We need to fort up right now."

He whipped his horse and raced to the first wagon. Kathleen watched him motion to the men in that wagon to stop, but the wagon rumbled on. She saw Holtz and Billy Gap Tooth stretch their lead to sixty yards ahead of the first wagon.

The pitch of the war cries swelled. She looked back and saw the Comanche break into a charge. She looked ahead. Holtz and Billy lashed their horses into a dead run, leaving the wagons on their own. Colter waved and shouted again at the first wagon, but its men whipped up their team to chase after the two fleeing mountain men. Colter tossed a glance over his shoulder. Then he swung his horse well out from the flight of the wagons and the pursuing Indians.

"The rifle!" Kathleen cried at George Croftin, who clung to a sideboard of the wagon bed. "The captain can't drive and shoot at the same time. Get the rifle!"

The man tore his gaze away from the oncoming Comanche long enough to seize the long rifle. He aimed out the back of the wagon at the Comanche still a hundred yards away and coming on in a weaving, swirling charge. The barrel of the flintlock bounced with every jolt of the careening wagon. The teamster fired and missed. The Comanche war cries took on a taunting eagerness, and the Indians broke straight for the wagon.

As the Comanche pulled even with the wagon, Kathleen froze with terror. The warriors' faces and chests were painted in wild exotic patterns. Most of them shook lances or waved bows. The most fearsome looking Comanche pointed a rifle at the wagon ahead of them and motioned to the other Indians. Renewing the howling cries, twelve Comanche sped after the first wagon. Then the leader of the war band with three of his followers closed in on both sides of the wagon with Kathleen.

One of the Comanche leaped from his horse onto the side of the wagon and pulled himself into the wagon bed. George Croftin swung the rifle at the Indian like a club, but the Comanche ducked the barrel and grappled the teamster. An arrow flashed past Kathleen's face and buried itself in Captain Freepole's chest, and Kathleen screamed. The leader of the Comanche leaned from his horse and swept her off the buckboard seat in the crook of one arm. She struggled, but the arm around her waist was like iron. She managed to pull her left arm free while the Comanche bellowed in amusement. Her left hand went to the knife in her belt. She tore it free and sank it to the hilt in the Comanche's throat. Both of them pitched headlong from the horse.

Air knocked from her lungs by the shock of the fall, she lay stunned. Then she forced herself onto her hands and knees. She had to get away. She staggered to her feet and saw a Comanche bearing down on her with his lance leveled at her bosom. Knowing she could not outrun his horse, she stood still, trying to ready her shaking legs to dodge the lance head. A shot cracked, and the Comanche hurtled from his horse scant yards from her feet.

"THE HORSE!" James Colter hollered and galloped his mount toward her. She thought he had deserted her and the others. "Grab the reins! Don't let him get away!"

She limped to the dead leader's horse, a brown and cream paint. When the pony shied away, she lunged at the reins. She caught and held onto the braided rawhide, though the pony reared and fought her hold. The leather burned her palms, but she held on. Colter pulled up next to the paint and seized its wooden bit.

"Mount up!" Colter shouted and held the pony still. She let go of the reins, grabbed two fistfuls of the paint's mane, and heaved herself onto its bare back.

"Hang on!" Colter cried, swooped up the paint's reins in one hand and kicked his horse into a gallop. Kathleen clung to the pony's mane while Colter led them due south away from the massacre by the Arkansas.

Hours later, the sun went down, and still, Colter drove the two horses at a brutal pace. Kathleen had never ridden a horse. She had grown up in an Irish slum in Boston, her family too poor to ever own a horse. In the past, she had traveled by carriage or wagon but mostly her own two feet. Now, she held onto the paint's mane, though it stung her blistered palms. Her skirt was not cut for riding and hiked up above her knees. The relentless grind of the paint's sweat-slick flanks chafed the inside of her legs, and the horse's backbone pounded her with every stride.

A half moon climbed into the sky. Colter had not said a word since leaving the Arkansas far behind. He had tied the paint's reins to his saddle cantle to free both hands for his own reins and rifle. He scanned the prairie on all sides. Abruptly, he stopped the horses and dismounted.

"We'll walk the horses for a spell," he said. "They need a rest, but we have to keep moving."

She slid off the paint's back. When she tried to stand, her knotted leg muscles cramped. She leaned against the horse's side for support. Colter untied the pony's reins and let them fall from his saddle. He stared restlessly around the night prairie, hardly noticing Kathleen. Her throat felt caked with dust. Her tongue clung to the roof of her mouth, feeling thick and dry.

"Water?"

"Quiet!" Colter whispered. He looked at her a moment, unhooked the leather canteen hanging on his saddle, and held it out. She reached for it greedily, but he kept hold of it while she drank. After two swallows, he pulled it away.

"It's all we got. Got to save it. Let's move." He hung the water bag on his saddle and strode toward the southwest. Kathleen stumbled along behind him, clutching the paint's wooden bit for support. They walked about two hours. Her legs threatened to buckle with every step. The muscles in her back burned with strain. Colter strode along in front of her, studying the land and whispering to her to speed up her pace.

After two hours, he mounted his horse and motioned for her to climb on the paint. She struggled to mount and twice fell back. On the third try, she managed to hook enough of her upper body across the horse's back to swing her right leg over its back. She held her own reins this time. Colter was already twenty yards away. She hurried to catch up, despite the agony along her chafed legs.

They alternated riding and walking. A fitful wind out of the northwest set the buffalo grass rolling and swaying. As far as Kathleen saw in all directions, moonlight rippled and shimmered off endless waves of tossing stalks. Occasionally, a cloud scuttled across the sky like a huge ship sailing an ocean of stars. The swirling prairie grew hazy in her vision. She rode or trudged with her head down, hardly conscious of what she did, knowing only that she had to keep going. About two hours before dawn, Colter halted and swung down from his horse. She slid off hers and collapsed on her rump still clinging to the reins.

"Get some sleep." Colter unsaddled his mount. Kathleen let go of the reins and sank to the ground.

In what seemed less than a minute, a hand shook her left upper arm. She blinked open her eyes in the early morning sunlight, and then a bolt of fear snapped her wide awake. Colter's face was bent close to hers. She yelled and lashed out with her free

arm, but he clamped a calloused palm over her mouth and
pinned her down with his other arm.

CHAPTER 4

"Hush! Ain't got time for that now." When Kathleen quit struggling, Colter let go and stood up. "We got to put a heap of territory between us and them Comanche. They're bound to pick up our trail while they're picking over what's left of the others."

He stomped to his horse with anger still visible in his eyes. He pulled a dark chunk from a leather pouch tucked between his saddle and bedroll. When she struggled to her feet, he tossed the chunk to her. She caught and examined it while keeping an eye on Colter. The chunk was some sort of dried meat, and she realized how hungry she was, but the chunk was small. She bit off a corner. Dry and tough. She worked her jaws to chew it. Colter climbed aboard his horse. Still chewing the meat and wishing for a drink of water that Colter showed no inclination to offer her, she forced her aching muscles to mount the paint. Colter set off at a brisk pace toward the southwest. She followed, knowing she had no chance out here on her own. She wondered whether Colter meant to find "time for that." Now, even her knife was lost. She cursed herself for ever leaving St. Louis and wished hopelessly for a rifle.

About midmorning, Colter slowed, leaned far to one side and studied the ground. Then he nodded and straightened up.

"What is it?" she asked.

"Tracks."

"Comanche?"

"Nah, the hoofprints are shod." He set heels to his horse.

37

They rode for another hour, following the trail that only Colter saw. The tracks led southwest.

"It's them." Colter jerked his head toward the horizon. "Billy and German Joe."

She shaded her eyes and stared. After several moments, she picked out two mounted figures tiny in the distance.

"Do you intend to catch up with them?" She tried to hide the tremor in her voice. Persuading one, strange, violent, mountain man to guide her safely to Santa Fe was all the challenge she needed. Now, the difficulty would be tripled.

"Three rifles better'n one," Colter answered.

"But they were not anxious to use theirs back at the Arkansas."

"That's so," Colter said, "but they still got rifles and know how to use them."

They followed the two distant figures for another few minutes. When the mountain men stopped and turned around, Kathleen bit her lip. In another ten minutes, Colter and Kathleen trotted up beside the half-breed and Holtz.

"Well, looky here, Billy," Holtz brayed and pointed at Kathleen. "Colter's done brung the schoolmarm. Now, that's what I call right smart thinking."

"Just remember I brought her," Colter said.

"And just you remember me and Billy was free and clear of them Comanche, till ya'll no doubt swung them back on our trail." Holtz glared a moment at Colter and then said, "We's headed for cover in the hill country by the Purgatoire River. I expect that's your idea, too?"

"Yeah."

"Let's git on then," Holtz said and set out toward the west. Billy swung alongside Colter, who sidled his horse five yards away from the half-breed but kept even with him. Kathleen followed the three men with a sinking heart.

For seven more days, they fled across the prairie. They traveled all day and well into each night, stopping just long enough to let the horses crop grass. The little jerky in the three men's pouches ran out the second day, so they ate roots, grass, and lizards. Once, Billy caught a prairie dog. Afraid to risk a fire, they ate it raw. Kathleen wolfed down her share and wished for more. The vast flat openness of the Staked Plains exposed them to all eyes in range to see. The hands of the mountain men rested on the hammers of their rifles. Preoccupied with avoiding Comanche, they watched the skylines, not Kathleen, but she watched them and was grateful for the Comanche threat, so long as it stayed just a threat.

Though the sun baked the mountain men, it had long since weathered their flesh a wrinkled dark brown. Each wore a floppy wide-brimmed hat to shade his face. Kathleen had lost her bonnet in the fall from the Comanche leader's horse. A redhead, she had fair skin, well sprinkled with freckles but pale. Her face was sunburned and swollen. Her forehead and cheeks felt as if a swarm of hornets stung her. Her lips cracked. If she brushed sweat off her nose, the skin split open and bled. When they paused to slake the horses' thirst and refill the water bags at a small muddy hole, Colter jammed his felt hat on her head and turned away before she could thank him.

Seven days after the murder of Captain Freepole, the ground sloped gradually upward, and the men's faces took on an eager glint. They pressed forward. On the morning of the eighth day, a series of hills sprang up on the western skyline, but a slight dust cloud hung above the eastern horizon.

"We got to make them hills, if we hope to have a prayer of losing them Comanche," Holtz cried. They broke into a dead run toward the hills. They reached the first line of low, rounded hills while the dust cloud was still far to the east but closing. They raced over the first ridge and altered course toward the northwest. They twisted in and out of shallow gullies and among steadily rising hills, until the grass gave way to scattered mesquite and scrub oak. They slowed the foam-spattered horses to a walk and angled more sharply northwest. Coming upon a wide flowing stream, they dismounted to walk the spent horses up its length for several miles, letting the water hide their tracks.

"Good thing them Injuns are Comanche," Holtz said. "If they was Apaches, all this twisting and turning wouldn't amount to a hill of beans. Apaches'd track us to hell and gone without losing a minute wondering which way we went."

Billy Gap Tooth grunted in agreement. Colter just kept walking and watched the terrain. Kathleen followed, not knowing where the mountain men were going or why. She did know that Santa Fe was to the southwest.

When night came, they left the stream and rode for several miles through territory that angled steadily upward and blossomed with brush and scattered clumps of cottonwoods. Finally, the men hid in a stand of trees and made the horses lie down. Kathleen huddled against her pony's side for warmth. She dozed fitfully, afraid to sleep. The men ignored her and, rifles by their sides, sat listening to the sounds of the night.

They traveled like this for six more days. On the third day, they spotted the Comanche silhouetted on top of a ridgeline and hid in a narrow draw all day. On the fifth day, the white crests of the Sangre de Cristo Mountains loomed to the west beyond the hilltops. The men eyed those distant peaks. On the sixth day, the land dropped abruptly to the valley of the Purgatoire River. They rode down into the valley, forded the river, and climbed the valley's far side, pressing through hills now covered with dark spruce and pine. The land tilted sharply upward toward the mountains that soared higher against the sky.

As they climbed the outskirts of the mountains, the tension in Holtz and Billy Gap Tooth eased away, but Colter still rode with a certain distance from the half-breed and Holtz, as well as from Kathleen. She did not put much hope in that. Colter had always kept that distance.

"Best way to go is north of the Spanish Peaks through Sangre de Cristo Pass," Holtz said and watched Colter. "Comanche probably think we headed south to Raton Pass. Ain't seen nary a sign of them in two days. Once we get through the pass, we can mosey along the other side of the mountains to Taos Pueblo. We can hole up there safe. Them Pueblos been tamed by the Spanish for a heap of years."

"Good sense," Billy Gap Tooth grunted. These were the first words Kathleen had heard him speak since Upper Crossing. Colter nodded. Holtz looked at Kathleen and smiled. She tried not to show any emotion on her face. They headed deeper into the mountains, and Kathleen had to follow.

When they camped inside the pass north of the Spanish Peaks, the half-breed lit a fire, the first blaze the men had risked since the wagons were ambushed. Holtz ambled off into dense evergreen stands with his rifle. Within half an hour, Kathleen heard a shot farther up the valley. She looked at Billy and Colter. Neither showed concern. At sunset, Holtz tramped into camp carrying a slain mule deer fawn. He threw the carcass by the fire and skinned it. He cut off several hunks of meat, stuck them on long pointed sticks, and lodged the other ends of the sticks in the dirt by the fire. While this meat hung over the flames to cook, Holtz bent a sapling downwind of the fire and tied the top to another tree. He trimmed venison strips no thicker than a cracker from the carcass. These he hung on the bent sapling to smoke dry.

When the meat above the fire was done, each of the group pulled a sizzling venison-laden stick from the flames. The mountain men sliced off mouthfuls with their wide-bladed knives. Kathleen at first tried to bite off mouthfuls with her teeth, but the meat fell off the stick. She caught it in her hands, but hot grease seared her blistered palms. She let the meat fall on her lap. She would not beg for a knife.

"Here." Colter tossed his knife into the dirt next to her legs. She picked it up and cut the meat into bite-sized morsels, avoiding the eyes of the mountain men. When she finished, she stood up and extended the hilt to Colter. His eyes flared for the briefest instant, but he took the knife without a word. Kathleen licked her cracked lips. What had the flare of Colter's eyes meant, if anything?

At this elevation, the night air cooled far below the temperature of the prairie. The men loosened bedrolls and spread blankets on the ground. Kathleen crouched by the fire and hugged her knees.

"I got me a nice warm blanket." Holtz sighed. "You can sort of pay me the wages I'm owed by sharing it tonight. Don't reckon I'll collect none off ole Freepole."

"Captain Freepole has a brother in Santa Fe who minds the business at that end," Kathleen said. "I'm sure he will settle whatever debts the poor captain owed you."

"Why you figure he'd do that?" Holtz asked. Billy Gap Tooth watched her from across the fire.

"It was the brother's idea," Kathleen said, "to play up to the Mexican authorities by bringing in a good Catholic schoolteacher for his and their partners' children. As you might know, the Mexicans are very suspicious of Americans, especially Protestants like Freepole. By hiring me, his brother hoped to gain the favor of the Mexican governor. Since it was at his brother's suggestion that I was hired, Captain Freepole's brother is still bound to pay you—if I arrive there unharmed."

"Sounds mighty iffy to me." Holtz grinned. Colter pulled his rifle from behind his saddle and laid it beside him. Holtz's grin stayed, but the muscles stood out in his neck, and his eyes flicked back and forth between Kathleen and Colter.

"I'll be fine right here by the fire," she said.

"All right, but we got a long ways yet to go. You might find"— Holtz paused, cast a quick look at Colter, and then winked at Billy—"you'll have to change your mind."

Holtz and Billy settled down under their blankets. Soon Holtz snored, but the half-breed's eyes were open. Kathleen sneaked a peak at Colter. His saddle propped up his head and shoulders. A corner of his blanket covered the stock and action of his rifle. He watched Billy and German Joe and her, but she found no reassurance in Colter's cold blue eyes.

She looked away, toying with the idea of running away if Billy and Colter slept but rejected it. She had seen Colter track. And if she somehow did manage to lose them, what then? She would be without food, horse, or firearm. She knew only that Santa Fe lay somewhere to the southwest, but how far away and how to survive walking there alone she had no idea.

What would Colter do? She tried to think of a scheme to play him against Holtz and Billy. Every idea seemed ridiculous, but she had to think of something. Angry tears built in her eyes, and she fought them down. She looked again at Colter, tried to catch his eyes, but he watched Holtz and Billy Gap Tooth. So she huddled by the fire and kept it burning all night.

CHAPTER 5

In the morning, through weary eyes, Kathleen watched the men wake and stir about. Cold, aching, bruised, and scraped raw, she had not slept. Holtz and Billy wandered to the horses and loosened the hobbles, so the horses could graze farther from camp in daylight. Colter fiddled with his gear—checking shot bag, powder horn, and rifle. The men seemed in no hurry to travel. She feared what this meant for her, so she hid a rock under a fold of her skirt. Maybe, if she fought hard enough, they would have to kill her first. Then Holtz and Billy strode to the fire.

"Colter." Holtz stood with one hand loosely grasping his upper rifle barrel while his other forearm rested on the muzzle. Billy cradled his rifle across his chest with both hands. "Me and Billy reckon it's time to collect our wages. We don't put much faith in her words about no brother of Captain Freepole's paying us." Holtz's tone was light, reasonable but firm. "Can't say as money amounts to much with me, no ways. I'm thinking me and Billy's owed something all the same. She's a mighty fine hunk of woman and white to boot. Ain't had a white woman in a heap of years. Now don't go getting me wrong. Me and Billy ain't aiming to cut you out of what's owed you none. You brung her along from the Arkansas, and that's a fact. Me and Billy both agreed you got first rights. We'll holt her arms and legs while you go first. I don't reckon she'll scratch much after the night she's spent. What you reckon? That sound reasonable to you?"

"I reckon that sounds reasonable," Colter said, flung up his rifle, and shot Billy Gap Tooth through the heart.

Kathleen gasped, but Holtz leaped backward several yards to gain time to bring up his rifle. Colter sprang across the fire with a drawn knife in his right fist. He flung himself to one side when Holtz leveled the rifle. Holtz fired, and the ball creased the muscle running from Colter's neck to his left shoulder. Colter winced, gathered his feet, and rushed Holtz. Stumbling back, Holtz reversed his hold on the rifle and swung it like a club. Colter ducked back. The two men circled each other with Holtz murderously swinging the rifle back and forth while Colter looked for an opening to dodge past it. They were twenty yards from the fire.

Kathleen watched them from the other side of Billy Gap Tooth's corpse. His Hawken lay two yards from his body. She stared at it for an instant, then scrambled on hands and knees to where it rested. Still on her knees, she lifted the weapon, cocked the hammer, and tried to aim at Holtz's moving chest. The rifle was so heavy. She fought to hold the barrel steady. With her last strength, she pulled the trigger. The rifle fired and bucked against her shoulder like the kick of a mule. The recoil flung her on one side.

But the heavy fifty-four-caliber ball slapped Holtz's right shin and ripped the leg from under him. He was thrown on his side. Colter pounced, but Holtz heaved up on both knees and smashed the maple rifle stock against Colter's ribs. Colter grunted, dove on top of Holtz, and pinned him to the ground. Then Colter sank the knife in Holtz's belly.

"Reckon she's all yourn now," Holtz gasped.

"I reckon so!" Colter spat in Holtz's face and shoved the knife deeper in the other man's gut. Holtz's face twisted in a grimace and then went slack.

Rubbing her right shoulder, Kathleen sat up. The joint was sore and tender. Afraid it was separated, she eyed Colter, who wrenched the knife out of Holtz and stood up, kicking the corpse farther down the shallow slope. His arms and back trembled. His breath came in heaving pants. When he turned to regard her, his eyes blazed.

She reached over and picked up the half-breed's rifle. Clutching the rifle like a talisman, she stood up and edged away from Colter.

"You won't find that much use without his shot bag and powder horn," Colter snarled and strode to the gear by his saddle. He slashed a length of cloth from his blanket and jammed it on the red oozing crease on his shoulder.

Keeping an eye on Colter, she bent and stripped the half-breed's corpse of shot bag and powder horn. She thought a moment and then also took his knife. Blood soaked the corpse's chest and back. She wiped blood off the shot bag onto the half-breed's pant leg. She was glad Billy and Holtz were dead, and she was not ashamed at a twinge of satisfaction at helping kill them. She stepped over to the fire and watched Colter.

Anger still blazed white hot in his eyes. He stared at her for a few seconds and then stomped toward the grazing horses. Without a word, the two set about breaking camp. Kathleen collected Holtz's blanket, tinder box, and the jerky off the bent sapling. Colter saddled his horse and her paint, strapping two water skins to the saddles. He went about his tasks with a fury, frequently pausing to glare at the world and Kathleen. He stamped out the fire and turned to Kathleen.

"Mount up!"

Clinging to her heavy, but oh so precious rifle, she had trouble climbing aboard the pony. Colter snorted and tramped across to where Holtz's rifle lay on the ground. He seized it, strode to his horse and lashed it behind his saddle. Then he glared at Kathleen and looked away. His eyes had subsided to their cold blue tint.

"Utes or Apaches will find this campsite before long," he said. His tone was subdued, embarrassed, shy. "They're welcome to the two horses, but ain't no sense in leaving them a good Hawken."

They set off west up the pass, riding with Colter in the lead. Mindful of his last words to Holtz, Kathleen kept a little distance between the horses. Colter's restless eyes took in the terrain around him, but he glanced over his shoulder at Kathleen more than he ever had in the past. She watched him load his rifle, but his body shielded most of the operation from her sight. She tried to remember how to load her rifle but, unsure of the exact procedure, did not attempt the process on horseback. At least, she had Billy's knife.

The pain in her shoulder subsided to a dull ache. The joint was stiff, but she could flex it through the full range of motion. She decided it was just badly bruised, painful but not much to notice when added to the list of her other aches and injuries.

Colter set a slow pace, and after a while, Kathleen saw that he was fighting pain in his ribs. He voiced no complaint, but once when his horse stumbled on a root, she heard him suck in his breath through clenched teeth. In midafternoon, she called to him to stop.

"I thought you'd be in a hurry to get to Taos," he said.

"I won't get there if you drop dead way out here." She swung down from her horse. "Get off, and I'll take a look at your side."

"I ain't bellyaching."

"I never said you were. Now get off your horse."

He swung gingerly out of the saddle, favoring his left side. She told him to take off his buckskin shirt and sit down on a small boulder. But he couldn't raise his arms over his head, so she had to help him. An ugly purple bruise discolored the flesh on the left side of his rib cage. When she made him lift his left arm so she could examine the bruise, he winced. Exploring the ribs with her fingertips, she tried to be gentle. His eyes squinted shut, but he did not jerk away or cry out. The skin of his torso was pale white, except for a dark brown *V* extending down from his neck.

"I believe two of your ribs are cracked," she said. "I'm going to bind them. It will hurt a good deal, but you'll feel better once it's done."

He nodded. She looked down at her tattered dress and the remains of her single petticoat. Deciding he would not see any more than was already on display, she tore several long strips from the hems of both. She told him to let out his breath and hold it. When he did so, she wrapped the wide flat strips around his rib cage, pulled them tight to support the cracked ribs, and tied the bandages off on his other side.

An uneasy silence had grown up between them. They avoided each other's eyes.

"You sit here while I make camp," she told him and walked away.

The uneasy silence hung between them while she unsaddled the horses, built a fire, and spread blankets on opposite sides of the flames. From time to time, she glanced at him. He did not speak, but his eyes followed her. When she finished, he got off the rock and sat down with his back propped against his saddle. He pulled his blanket up to his neck. She set several venison strips on a rock and poured water on them to soften them.

After supper, they sat on opposite sides of the fire. Restless, she picked up her rifle, shot bag, and powder horn and attempted to load the gun. His eyes never left her.

"You don't have it quite right. You put in too little powder, didn't tamp it down, and forgot the patch entirely. Ball's just going to pop out the muzzle and fall at your feet. Here, let me show you."

She looked at him for several moments, but she could tell nothing from his expression. She decided, if necessary, she could always whack his injured ribs and run away. She carried the rifle and equipment around the fire and sat down beside him.

He took the rifle from her and slapped the barrel to dislodge the ball and powder. Then he picked up shot bag and powder horn. He unstoppered the powder horn and pulled a white patch from the shot bag. He handed these to Kathleen and then picked up the rifle.

"Count to at least three when you pour in the powder. This fifty-four's got a heavy ball and needs a goodly amount to throw it. It's too large a bore for a woman, even one big as you. Don't count anymore than five, or the barrel will burst. Next, take a patch and tamp it down with the rod to pack the powder tightly in place. Then drop in the ball, but be sure to tamp it down to make it sit snug against the powder charge. You got the part right about setting the cap on the anvil seat. Heap of folks forget that and end up in a sorry fix when they least need to. See if you can do it right."

He handed her the rifle. She laid it across her lap and followed his instructions. When she finished, he nodded approval. The tension dropped back in place between them. She was a little ashamed of herself but could not forget his last words to Holtz.

"Your English is much better than most of the men I've met out west," she said to break the silence.

"My Pa was an undertaker back in Maryland." Colter sighed. "He meant for me to take over the business one day. Made sure I got plenty of schooling, so's I'd talk proper and dignified like a good undertaker. Some of it took. Some didn't."

"You're certainly the furthest thing from an undertaker."

"I couldn't stand those damn boxes." Eyes hot with pain, he stared at the flames and then rolled over on his uninjured side, away from her. She crept back to the opposite side of the fire and lay down with the rifle beside her.

In the morning when they broke camp, she asked how far away Taos was. He told her it was a very long day's ride, but they could make it if they pressed on without delay. Then he touched heels to his horse. Since they were well out of the pass, they headed south along the western side of the mountains. The silence was there between them again, and she intended to let it stay. She could almost feel the inside of the adobe walls at Taos Pueblo. She had not slept inside the walls of a house in many long weeks. Perhaps, she could even take a bath. She had not had a real bath since leaving St. Louis.

Colter held himself stiffly in the saddle but pushed the pace. By the set of his jaw, Kathleen knew he was in a good deal of physical pain. But a deep, haunted, inward turning pain in his eyes seemed to drag him onward. In Taos, she told herself, he could find proper attention and rest, but after riding for three hours, she told him to stop and let her retie the bandages. He halted his horse and sat rigid in the saddle waiting for her to catch up.

"I expect I'd best get you along to Taos," he said without turning his head when she rode up beside him. The skin of his face stretched taut trying to mask the pain.

"Well, I'd better re-wrap those bindings before we go any farther," she said and climbed off her horse. He dismounted with a grunt. She had him hold up his shirt.

"Maryland, that's where you're from?" she asked while she untied the loose bandages. He nodded and winced. How pale the flesh of his chest was. How smooth. "I taught school for three years in Baltimore," she said. The fingers of her right hand lay across the edge of his stomach muscles where they met the ribs. Warmth flooded her face. "Was that anywhere near your home?"

"Nah, I grew up in Hagerstown, long way west of Baltimore," he answered. "That's where I first knew the Hawken brothers, Samuel and Jacob. Their pa was a gunsmith there. He was a close friend of my pa's. Jacob insisted my pa bury his father when the smallpox killed him."

"I thought those were smallpox marks on your cheeks," she muttered, glad to have something to distract her while her hands wrapped the bandages around his rib cage. "I assume you caught it about the same time?"

"Whole town damn near died of it." His eyes were misty and far away with memory. The cold tint was gone. In its place was a dim pain, like barely glowing coals taken out of a fire pot after the night to rekindle the morning blaze. "I caught it at the very first. Ma caught it tending me and my two sisters. It killed Ma and my sisters."

"And your father, did he die of it, too?" She knotted the last binding in place.

"He died, too," Colter said and looked away. It was as if she had blown on the coals. His eyes burned hot with pain. Kathleen stared at him a moment, afraid she had pried too deeply. She wanted to put her hand on his shoulder but, instead, turned and climbed on her paint.

He seemed to ride more comfortably but kept the pace at a slow, easy walk. She still wondered why he had said what he had to Holtz, but she had no more fear of him. She watched him carefully. Ignoring her and the terrain around him, he looked at his horse's neck, but his eyes were unfocused, pain-filled, trapped. After several hours, he rode with his head bowed and his eyes clinched shut. His elbows were pressed close to his sides, but whenever his horse paused to crop grass, Colter's eyes flared open just long enough for him to jerk the reins and to kick the horse's flanks. Then his eyes clamped shut again. She thought about the adobe walls at Taos and sighed.

"We'll camp here for the night." She grabbed the reins of his horse. He glanced at her, nodded, and let his head sink back on his chest. Intending to help him dismount, she climbed down from her horse, but he slid off the far side of his mount away from her and made his way to a spruce stump. He sat down against the stump with his face drained of color. She made camp.

He fell asleep propped against the spruce stump while she prepared supper. From some nearby bushes, she collected a pile of blackberries in his felt hat. She laid out several strips of venison on rocks and moistened them. Then she stepped over to wake Colter. His color was better, and the strain lines were gone from around his eyes and mouth. This was the first time she had ever seen him at peace—free of the wariness, free of pain. She wanted to freeze that peace on his face, make it her gift for his waking hours. She admitted to herself the attraction and that terrified her.

She stood again a little girl of three outside her mother's bedroom door, listening to the birthing screams. At six years, she was inside the room helping her aunts midwife her mother. She saw again the deep lines in her mother's sweat-soaked face, heard her gasp, and wiped the blood from her thighs. Each birth, there was more blood, staining the sheets, the midwives' clothes, and the rags that Kathleen used to wipe it away. The room stank of blood. It smothered her. She gagged and vomited, and the vomit was colored red. At twelve, she had asked her mother why. Because of love, her mother had said.

A brown pine needle fell onto Colter's face. She knelt beside him and brushed it away. His eyes opened. The lines furrowed around eyes and mouth. The skin became taut.

"Supper," she said. He walked to the fire without her assistance and sat down with his back against his saddle. She sat down next to him. He picked at the meat but hungrily munched the berries. She ate her food and watched him. He pushed the half finished portion of venison away, slumped against the saddle, but looked much stronger.

"Why did you say what you did to Holtz when you killed him?"

"Guess I just wanted to send him to hell thinking he'd been outsmarted," he said and stared at the ground. His eyes were hard, cold, metal, and that filled her with a confused and frightened despair. "I didn't mean to scare you."

"I was afraid you meant to . . ."

He raised his head and looked at her. His eyes had shed the closed, wary mask. The blue eyes were open, desperate, and vulnerable.

"I'm not that kind of man," he said.

She breathed a silent prayer, leaned forward, and kissed him, smearing most of the kiss across his chin. Then face hot and red, she drew back from him, feeling silly and fighting back tears that welled up from embarrassment and passion—tears that turned to anger.

"Damn you! Damn you to hell!"

He stared at her for a moment. Then he reached out his right hand and grasped her left shoulder, but when he bent forward to kiss her, his face twisted in pain, and he sank back with a gasp against his saddle. She took his right hand and held it until the color came back to his face.

"I'm all right," he said.

"James," Kathleen said, savoring the sound of his name on her tongue, "you're the biggest liar west of St. Louis."

CHAPTER 6

That night, she lay with her head close enough to his saddle to reach out and touch him if there was need. He smelled of sweat-stained leather and horseflesh, but the smell of sweat and horses clung to her, too. She daydreamed about taking a bath with him, soaping his neck and chest with lather while he toyed with her breasts. Once, he woke them both with a gasp. Flinging off her blanket, she squatted on her heels beside him.

"Are you all right?" Her left hand felt his forehead—warm, a bit feverish. Her right hand hovered above his chest, afraid to touch him, afraid not to. She batted at a long strand of her hair that hung above his face.

"My sisters had hair the color of yours," he said. "But they were just four—twins they were—when the smallpox broke out. Still had that fine, soft baby hair. I was fifteen at the time. Prettiest brace of girls I've ever seen. They used to follow me around, begging me to play with them or tell them stories. I didn't mind. Used to tell them the biggest whoppers I could think of, just to see their faces shine.

"Then they got sick with the smallpox. Ma died pretty fast, but I started to get better. Pa went right on with his undertaking. Pretty near buried everyone we knew. Always did a bang up job, real solemn and dignified. Folks kept dying, and Pa kept right on sticking them in those boxes. He put Ma in a fine oak casket and buried her. It drove me near crazy. He wanted me to help him, but I refused. He yelled and threatened, but I

54

wouldn't do it. Pa was sick by then, too sick to beat me. Then the girls died. Pa dragged them downstairs and laid them in their tiny coffins.

"Sickness does funny things to your thinking. I tore around the house near out of my mind. I couldn't stand the thought of those beautiful little girls trapped inside them boxes. I ran downstairs screaming at Pa. He had collapsed next to the worktable that held the twins' coffins. He begged me to finish the job. Instead, I pried the lids off those boxes and dumped the bodies on the table. Pa started yelling I was damned forever. I just laughed and turned over all the chemical jars with the preservatives. Dragged Pa out in the yard. Then I set fire to the whole house and burned them all to ashes. I cried with joy when the ashes floated up into the sky, free as birds."

She wanted to lay her head on his chest and wrap her arms around his body; instead, she had to untie his bandages, pull them snug even though he cried out, then tie the knots tight again. Then she had to scramble up and find a cloth to wet so she could wipe his face and neck. "What happened to you?"

"Oh, nothing much. Pa died the next day raving." He sighed. "Folks was too worried about smallpox to try and figure out what happened. I had to live with some relatives over in Frederick for a while, but I ran away. They brought me back, but I kept running away, until they quit looking for me. I was sixteen then. I took to drifting west. Doing this and that. Couldn't stand to live close to people for long. All the rules and laws just seem like another kind of box.

"Out here, there ain't any boxes. Most Indians don't even bury their dead. Instead, they stick them on raised platforms and let the birds eat 'em. No coffins at all. Except the Kiowas. They bury their dead just like white men. Weep and wail and carry on just like white men, too, but they're a small tribe. Can't figure why the Comanche ever hooked up with them.

Comanche don't set much store by that trash. Hell, they don't even believe in God. And they don't mind dying 'cause they think death's just a time to rest before starting a brand new life all over. Wouldn't mind coming back as a Comanche."

She wiped sweat off his chest, and when he winced, she bit her lip and silently cursed her hands. Tomorrow, she had to get to Taos and find help. If he could ride, fine. Otherwise, she would have to leave him and hope that she could find the Pueblo town and make herself understood. Would any of the Indians speak Spanish or English? But that was tomorrow. She had to get him through this night. "Sleep, James. Go to sleep now."

He looked up at her, smiled, and closed his eyes. She watched him a while longer, wiping sweat off his face every now and again. When his ragged breathing eased in slumber, she lay down beside him and pulled the blanket over them both. Her last night with him—alone. Finally, she slept.

About first light, she awakened. Colter was still asleep, but when she tried to slip out of the blankets without disturbing him, his eyes jerked open. With a grunt, he rolled over and heaved himself up, staggering a bit at first. She fussed at him to be still and rest while she built the morning cook fire, but he set about packing his bedroll. His color was better, so she hushed and squatted by the fire, wrapping the last of their jerky strips around two sticks to warm. When the meat was ready, she looked up and held out his portion. His eyes were cold again, closed down tight, shut against her. But not, she knew, against just her, rather against the whole world. Perhaps, she guessed, even against himself. She knew all about shutting off feelings, walling them away. Only somehow, hers had gotten free. But she knew nothing about breaking through such walls, just how to build them.

When Colter turned away and sat down to munch his food,

she reached for her blanket, rolled it up, and looked around for something to lash it tight. She decided to cut a strip off the empty food pouch. But while she did this, she nicked her left thumb with Billy's knife. She stared at the slight cut. It oozed barely two drops of blood. She started to weep.

Colter came quickly over and sank down on his knees in front of her.

"It don't look like much," he said. "I'm sure it will be all right."

"It doesn't hurt." She wiped a hand across her face. But she did hurt, more than she had hurt in a long, long time. A hurt as bad as when at twelve years old she had watched her mother bleed through another childbirth—the last one, the one that killed her. This was a hurt too strong to bear alone. She reached out and placed both hands on his face.

He stared at her a moment—a wild stare full of want and terror and self-hatred. Then he flung himself to his feet, staggered to the horses, and began saddling them. She bit her lip and studied his back. Jamming the sheathed knife under the bedroll lashings, she collected her rifle and shot bag and walked over to him.

"How long do you think it is to Taos?" she said to the small of his back. He cinched the paint's girth and spoke without looking at her.

"Half a day, I reckon. We'd best get started. Morning's near gone."

They tied the rest of their gear to the saddles, mounted, but sat their horses without moving. She studied his face. Finally, he looked directly at her. His eyes were cold and blue. He was a strong man. He had come a long way carrying his secret hell. He was used to the weight. Last night, she told herself, was past. She must put those emotions back behind their walls.

"James, about Billy's rifle?" she asked.

"Trade it in Santa Fe for another," he told her, and the hint of a smile slipped across his face. "A thirty caliber about do you, but make damn sure it's a Hawken."

★ ★ ★ ★ ★

PART II
NEW MEXICO

★ ★ ★ ★ ★

CHAPTER 7

Father Reynaldo was a tall, slim man in his mid-forties with the erect carriage of a gentleman of good family, but without the joyous zeal Kathleen expected from a Franciscan; rather, the knowledge that life had bypassed him shadowed his brown eyes. At Taos Pueblo, he welcomed Kathleen and Colter into his tiny mission of St. Jerome . . . nothing more than a squat, thick-walled, adobe building topped with a log cross, one long rectangular room for the sanctuary, a much smaller squared room for the priest's cell, and behind the church a three-walled shed for a burro and four sheep.

Father Reynaldo gave up his room to Kathleen, laid out straw pallets for Colter and himself in the animal shed, and sent an Indian messenger to the brother of Captain Freepole in Santa Fe. Kindness distinguished all of his treatment of Kathleen and Colter, the silent Pueblo children at his mission school, and their suspicious parents. However, an air of certainty that nothing ever came of his faithful service tortured a kindness that was both instinctive and refined by family traditions of gentility and his Franciscan education. Indeed, when Kathleen looked into Father Reynaldo's eyes for the first time, an urge to comfort the priest, to assure him that he was all right, that things had to work out for the best someday disconcerted her.

Over the course of the next week, she grew used to the tug of this feeling as she helped him care for Colter, clean the sanctuary, and tend the burro, sheep, and horses. Before the week was half gone, it had pulled her into helping him teach the Pueblo children. She was a better teacher than Father Reynaldo, even though he spoke as many European languages and had mastered Tewa Pueblo. But children spoke up in her classroom, laughed while they played games outside in the dusty fields, and cried, "Good bye! Good bye!" in Spanish to her before racing each other home; soon, he stood back with a faint smile branding his face—a new guilt to add to the one she carried together with Colter but could not share.

For guilt filled Colter with that wariness that made him silent and withdrawn, and she felt that guilt rising in her, no matter how undeserved and no matter how much she longed to tell him it did not matter, that nothing mattered to her but him. But that guilt strangled the small words of greeting when she brought him a bowl of breakfast porridge, even though she made herself look Colter squarely in the eyes. It kept her lips dumb when she wiped and combed her painted Comanche war pony and Colter's big roan, though no more than five feet away he sat on a stool smoking a pipe Father Reynaldo loaned him. And that undeserved agonizing guilt clinched her fists behind her back and made her stand aside each day while Father Reynaldo unwrapped the bindings on Colter's rib cage, traced with his fingers the outline of Colter's injured ribs beneath the pale white flesh, and then re-wrapped the bindings.

And on Friday, at the end of just one week at Taos Pueblo, after dismissing the children at the door of the sanctuary, when she saw Father Reynaldo walk around the corner of the adobe church with the pipe he had loaned Colter, guilt froze her legs and mouth. He held up the pipe.

"He's gone." He studied her a moment, afternoon sunlight sparkling off flecks of grey stubble on his chin. "I told Mr. Colter he ought to stay, at least until his ribs fully healed, but he said he needed to ride north before fall set in. 'It comes early,' he said, 'in the mountains where the beaver are thickest.' He needed summer to scout the streams for dead falls and snares. This late in the year, he might not find a fur trader in Rancho Taos to stake him, and without metal traps, he said it would take a lot more work to bring in a decent cache of pelts this winter. I said he ought to wait and say goodbye to you after school. He shook his head and said, 'Time to move on.' "

She nodded. He looked at her, ready to offer the comforts of his office and his kindness, but Kathleen trusted in his certainty of his own futility. After an awkward second or two, he sighed, patted her on the shoulder, and with that sad resigned smile on his face strode into the church. Only then did she grit her teeth and summon tears of anguished rage.

"You signed that contract with my brother, not me." Folding his arms across his chest, Roger Freepole squinted at Kathleen in the midday desert sun. His green eyes were close set, under bushy dark eyebrows flecked with grey. His face was narrow with large ears pressed flat against his skull, offset by dangling jowls and thin pursed lips. "You tell me that Benjamin's dead. End of contract, plain as day."

Standing in the doorway to the sanctuary, with her pupils bowed over their shared slates behind her, Kathleen scowled at Freepole. Twenty yards behind Freepole, his escort of bored Mexican lancers slouched in the scorching heat. A little apart from the common soldiers, their commander stood with a riding crop in his left hand dusting his gold braided uniform with a white handkerchief. He paused a moment to appraise Kathleen and then resumed dusting his uniform. A surge of blood heated her face. Father Reynaldo had sent messengers to Santa Fe eleven days ago. Her Comanche pony already answered to the new name she had given him, Banshee. And only now, Captain Freepole's brother Roger showed up at Taos

Pueblo to tell her this?

By God, the detestable little toad would learn not to trifle with Kathleen O'Dwyer! Hands on hips, she took a step closer to Freepole. A short man, he had to crane his neck to look at her, as she intended. She was all teacher now, filled with implacable righteousness.

"Was not Captain Freepole," she asked in Spanish, "your business partner?"

"Well, yes." Roger Freepole shifted to Spanish, as well, but his squint widened just a tad. He looked her up and down, despite the wedding band on his left hand. Oh, Kathleen knew his kind. Unlike bolder men, he would never say one forward word, never dare to slip an arm around her waist when no one watched. Yet he eyed her legs, her hips, her bosom, and lust darted out as anger. As if he found her body an assurance of weakness, he met her eyes again. She glared right back, and his eyes dropped to her breasts. When he looked up, his squint was harsher, his jaw thrust forward, his lips more pursed. "But I did not sign the contract. Your agreement was strictly between you and my brother. I had no part in it."

"It was all your idea." Kathleen took another step forward, and like a bullying student she had caught on the playground, Freepole stepped back, stumbling off the raised church porch, drawing laughter from the lancers, children peeking from within the church, even a smile from Father Reynaldo. "You proposed this contract. You convinced Captain Freepole to hire me. You told him that a good Catholic school teacher for your Protestant children was just the ticket to curry the governor's favor over the other American traders in Santa Fe. This was all your grand scheme. This was all lock, stock, and barrel part of your business partnership with your brother—'plain as day.'"

Face red, Freepole stood his ground. Sputtering, he shouted in English, "S-So you say. That just makes it your word, a woman's word, against mine, a respected merchant and family man. And what kind of woman are you? Riding in here, from what I hear tell, with just a brute mountain man for company. Demanding I honor a contract that I ain't even seen, much less signed." Looking around at the soldiers, he winked and then said in Spanish, "We all know what sort of contract women sign in St. Louis."

Father Reynaldo put a restraining hand on Kathleen's elbow, but she shook it off while the soldiers leered. Oh, the dastardly evil of the man! Taking everything she had suffered on her trip—Comanche attacks, starvation, exhaustion, a barely escaped rape at the hands of German Joe and Billy—and twisting them into a joke for other men as small and foul and obscene as Freepole. Damn them! Damn them all. Yes, all men who laughed and leered and looked at her as if she were the one ready to lie, to cheat, to throw away honor for a few moments of scratching lust. Men, cowards all! Who jumped their horses and rode away without so much as a goodbye, a backwards glance. Off on the next grand adventure. While she—

"Silence!" The commanding officer of the lancers roared at his men, who snapped upright on their mounts. Now, twirling his riding crop, he strode across the packed brown grit of the street and halted with a thud of his boot heels on the porch in front of Freepole. The porch's elevation adding to his imposing height, he towered above Freepole. "You have insulted a brave, eloquent, and may I say, beautiful lady. Though you are an unworthy and ill-spoken pig, you will beg her forgiveness."

"B-But—"

The officer laid his riding crop across Freepole's shoulder. At Freepole's bulging eyes, grins broke out on the lancers' faces. "Y-Yes sir. I mean, your excellency." His face's red shade deepened, and the lancers burst into renewed laughter until a glance from the commander silenced them. Humiliated fury filled Freepole's eyes. "Miss O'Dwyer. I apologize. I did not mean to insult you."

"You are a liar, but an obedient one." The officer tapped his riding crop on Freepole's shoulder. "You will, of course, honor the terms of the contract as Miss O'Dwyer recalls them." Tap. "After her ordeal in the prairies and mountains, no gentleman would expect her to have miraculously preserved something as inconsequential as a piece of paper." Tap. "Now, go wait with the horses where your ill-breeding will not offend the lady any further." The riding crop pointed the way.

Stiff-legged, fists clinched, Freepole lurched through the knot of grinning soldiers and across the street toward the horses hitched in front of South House, one of the two sprawling adobe buildings that made up Taos Pueblo. Halfway there, he cast a look at Kathleen that promised revenge. Then the lancers' officer doffed his plumed hat in an elaborate bow executed with the effortless grace of long practice.

"May I introduce myself?" he said and, with a click of heels, stood erect. His eyes were dark, but fiery, unlike Father Reynaldo's, which regarded him with a look of cool appraisal. The officer's posture carried the precise amount of tension to convey strength, grace, power. "I am Colonel Miguel Esteban Alvarro de Montoya, the new commander of his excellency our governor's garrison at Santa Fe. I crave the lady's pardon and beg her to allow me to offer my service as a gentleman. Had I the slightest inkling that Mr. Freepole would dare such effrontery I would have ordered him bound and gagged."

Kathleen gritted her teeth against a flood of invective. She wanted nothing more than to slap the waxed mustachios off Colonel Montoya's face. She ached to smash him and every man around her, including the good Father Reynaldo, into tiny bloody remnants of their puffed up male selves. Control, Kathleen, she told herself. Control. This man offered both an apology and assistance. He was the governor's second in command.

"I hold no grudge against you, Colonel Montoya," she said and nodded in Freepole's direction, "for the hateful and appalling behavior of my own countryman. I hope that you will not take his rudeness as typical of all Americans." There she had done it, matched him eloquence for eloquence, though she would be damned before she would stoop to a curtsey for his graceful bow.

"I assure you, Miss O'Dwyer, that you banish all such images from my mind." His Spanish was high born Castellón, deep and unwavering, as were his dark eyes. "I have come to offer you an escort to Santa Fe, where his excellency the governor is most anxious to hear the tale of your miraculous adventures. We will leave, if it suits the lady, in the morning. And if the lady is as kind as she is beautiful, she will grace me first with this tale on our journey to the capital."

A prickling ran along Kathleen's spine. What was a Spaniard, obviously of noble family and rearing, doing in a backwater province of Mexico, years after it had broken with the Spanish crown? She must watch Colonel Montoya carefully, and not simply because he was, yes, a handsome man.

That evening, through the narrow unglassed window of her small room, a soft, cool breeze out of the mountains to the northwest set the candle flame dancing. The thick adobe walls were still warm with the searing desert heat of the day, so Kathleen was grateful for the breeze. Any other night, she would have sat with Father Reynaldo on the church porch in the cool night air. He had loaned her a spare Franciscan robe of rough wool for the cold nights, and she would wear it while she mended her torn calico dress and tattered cotton underthings. Most nights, he asked her about America—what life was like in

Boston, in New York, in Baltimore. He had never been to America and listened attentively.

In turn, he told her about Spain and his own family. Although the family's Andalusian holdings were small, his was a proud family that traced its lineage to one of the Cid's most faithful knights. He had two brothers. By tradition inheriting the family title and lands, his older brother, Antonio, a short, fat, jolly man who loved his wife, his hearth, and his glass of red wine, had led a quiet life as a provincial baronet until Napoleon Bonaparte forced Spain to accept his own brother as its king. Then Antonio had taken to the mountains with his peons to fight this French stain upon Spanish honor. After years of struggle, Antonio rose to the rank of general in the rebel army that helped drive the French from Spanish soil and, in the process, lost a leg but never an ounce of fat from his belly. Then he returned home where his loving wife plied him with kisses and red wine, and his neighbors erected a statue of him in the town square. Father Renaldo's younger brother, Ramon, a slender man of medium height who as a boy had cried at a rabbit's bloody corpse when their father first took them hawking, had by tradition gone to the royal army. Young Ramon had soldiered throughout South America, fighting Indians and English raiders and rising steadily through the officer ranks. In his early thirties as a colonel of a cavalry regiment, he had fought the rebel San Martin to a standstill on the plains of Argentina. Promoted to general and transferred to Peru, he had driven the armies of Bolivar back into Colombia, where Ramon had nearly died of cholera. Recovering his health slowly in Cuba, he had married the viceroy's most beautiful daughter and was now marquis of a rich Cuban sugar plantation. Smiling faintly, Father Reynaldo said, "And I, the middle son, who as a youth loved the feel of a sword in my hand and horse between my legs, was by tradition given to the service of Holy Mother Church."

Then he told her about New Mexico, mostly about Taos and the Pueblos, how they mistrusted him and all other white men. When the native priests—and he called them priests, not medicine men or witches—led the ancient puberty dances in the public square and held the sacred, but outlawed, Kachina rituals in the pueblo's underground kivas, he did not send for lancers from Santa Fe, as other Catholic priests had done.

"If we had asked only for their souls, freely given, not conquered," he once said, "many of them would have embraced the one true Church, but you cannot demand that a people surrender everything they are, yet we Spanish demanded, and now these Mexicans, too, demand that these people give up their native tongue, their tribal leaders, their very selves. Three hundred years of bitter memories are all these people have from us, and bitterest of all are the memories of Taos Pueblo. Here began the Great Rebellion that freed New Mexico for many years from Spanish rule, and it was here, when Don Diego de Vargas retook the province, the conquistadores wrecked their worst vengeance. Taos was the center of the Pueblo world. The people were safe from outsiders behind their doorless adobe walls. What need had they for doors? They climbed ladders and descended into their homes through holes in the flat roofs. When the Apache, envious of the Pueblos' wealth, raided Taos, the peaceful citizens pulled up the ladders, and the Apaches soon learned the people of Taos were beyond their reach." Father Reynaldo sighed.

"Now, it is a dusty forgotten hole in a long neglected province. For conquistadors needed doors to enforce their strange laws, so the people of Taos cut the exact number of doors into South and North Buildings the outsiders' law said they must. Now, the Apaches raid with impunity, despite all my prayers. But the people of Taos attend Mass once a week because it is the law. They bring their children for me to baptize because it is the law. They send their children to my church school because it is the law. Then they go about their lives as they wish, and nothing the law or I say will ever change them."

But tonight, Kathleen sat on the little cot in her room and packed her gear. She had washed her patched dress and petticoats and hung them on a line tied across one corner of the room. In the morning, she would iron them with a flat heated rock. Still, she would look like a gringo pauper to the women of well-to-do Mexican families in Santa Fe, and to the wives and daughters of the American traders, she would be, in her patches and rags or borrowed Pueblo dresses, another Irish tramp.

She studied her Hawken rifle that leaned against the wall within easy reach. Firelight reflected along its oiled barrel and stock. Standing up, she fitted the butt of the rifle stock against her shoulder and sighted along the barrel. Since Colter's abrupt departure, she had practiced loading and firing the weapon every morning and found she had a marksman's knack for squeezing the trigger and riding the massive slamming recoil. At two hundred yards, she could hit a man-sized target one out of every two shots. Mountain man fashion, she rested the rifle across her body in the crook of her arm. Let the women of Santa Fe take the measure of that. And the men, too.

Then came a knock on the door.

"Kathleen?" Father Reynaldo's voice. She faced the door.

"Come in, Father."

The door swung open, and Father Reynaldo took a step into the room. Head tilted to one side, he regarded Kathleen, his eyes lingering on the rifle. Then head erect, he gazed at her face. A brightness, odd for him, filled his eyes. Gone, too, was the faint weary smile of resignation. His jaw was set, lips pressed tight. Kathleen's breath caught for a moment at this glimpse of a Father Reynaldo as he once must have been—sure of himself, handsome, regal. How the years had changed him so! God, what had happened to her? The man was a priest, and here she gawked at him as if he were some prince come to court her. What a child she had become! Damn you, James Colter. Damn you.

"Please reconsider going to Santa Fe," Father Reynaldo said. "You would be better off here."

Kathleen hugged the rifle with both arms. "Do not worry about the children, father. You are a learned and gentle teacher."

"But not a good one, you kindly do not say." The familiar weary smile touched his lips for a moment, but then determination surged redoubled across his face, lighting his eyes. "The children love you. They learn far more from you than I could ever teach them. But that is not why I wish that you would stay when Mr. Freepole departs in the morning."

"Father, I'm not worried about Roger Freepole." Kathleen laughed, a sharp nervous laugh. She took the rifle in one hand and shook it. "I won't even need this to handle the likes of that milk-boned coward."

Father Reynaldo turned and shut the door. Kathleen's fingers tightened on the rifle. Then he strode across the narrow room, robe brushing Kathleen's hand that clutched the rifle. On the other side of the room, he closed the wooden shutters of the window, and then arms folded on his rope belt, he faced her.

"I share your contempt for Mr. Freepole." The light in Father Reynaldo's eyes turned fierce. "Colonel Montoya, however, is of grave concern."

"What do you know of Colonel Montoya?" She fought to keep shock, yes, and anger out of her voice. Shock at the image of the handsome lancer flaring in her mind. Anger at Father Reynaldo. Jealousy? In a priest? Shock at her surge of pleasure. Anger at Father Reynaldo, Montoya, Colter. Where were all of these emotions coming from? A child. She had become a child.

"Nothing." Father Reynaldo stood a moment, glaring. Then he shook his head and sighed. The old weary smile crept onto

his face. He shook his head again. Straightening, shoulders
flung back, he put his hands on his hips and met her eyes.
"Everything. I have never met him before today, never heard a
word of his existence, but I know him, as I know the blood that
courses in my veins."

Then his eyes softened, filled with a sad warmth. He sat down
on the cot and motioned to her. "Put the rifle down, child. Sit
with me. I will tell you what I know of this Colonel Miguel Esteban Alvarro de Montoya."

Fighting the trembling that shook her grasp on the rifle,
Kathleen stood a moment longer. Then with a clumsy bang, she
leaned the rifle against the wall beside the head of the cot and
sat down, all too aware of the scant inches between them. How
could her emotions betray Colter this way? Yet hadn't he
betrayed her? So why did what she felt now for Father Reynaldo
and for Colonel Montoya fill her with this awful guilt? Why did
she feel any of this at all for Father Reynaldo, a man of God,
and Colonel Montoya, a man with whom she had only briefly
spoken? Guilt and pleasure jumbled together. Any attempt to
focus on one emotion, sort through it to some kind of resolution, strayed into unexpected and dizzying whirlpools of the
other.

"Colonel Montoya is a Spaniard of noble family." Father
Reynaldo folded his hands in his lap. He stared at the wall in
front of him. "As am I. Montoya is an old family name in
Castile, and although I am Andalusian, like knows like. We
share the same background, the same traditions, the same sense
of honor. We are filled with the same ambitions—the same
dreams of glory, of conquest. This is why I fear what may happen if you go to Santa Fe." He looked at her. "Mexico fears
them, too, those conquistador dreams of conquest and glory.
That is why in 1822, the government banned all pure-blooded
Spanish from the country, even those born in Mexico. How

Colonel Montoya avoided exile, I do not know, but this only adds fuel to my concern."

"But, Father, you are pure-blooded Spanish, as well," Kathleen said. "How did you avoid the ban?"

Father Reynaldo gazed at the dirt floor. He stirred the brown dust in a swirl with the toe of his sandal. "I didn't avoid it. God save me, I prayed for it as my salvation." The old weary resignation filled his eyes, leaving his face a remnant of his former assurance. His was still a handsome face, but it was a worn down beauty, like a windswept mansion abandoned in the midst of a desert. "But in Mexico City, there is an old Mestizo bishop who has not forgotten that a young priest, so proud of his noble Spanish lineage, so full of grand ambitions, was once his rival for high position in the church. He finds this backwater parish best suited to restrain whatever dreams of glory still trouble the priest from a wealthy and powerful Spanish family."

Kathleen knotted her hands together in her lap, fighting the urge to put a hand on top of Father Reynaldo's left hand, the fine, long-boned hand of an aristocrat, spotted with liver marks from the sun, encrusted with calluses of peasant life in Taos. Yes, hers would be a comforting hand, but she knew not an innocent one. And she feared, mistrusted, yet wanted the contact of his flesh.

"Do dreams, do they . . . still tempt you, Father?" There, she had asked it. Hands bound together in her lap, knee locked against knee, her lips still had asked. Try as she might to speak calmly, the tremor had been there in her voice. Head thrown back, he looked at her for a moment. Then a smile full of warmth and kindness crossed his face, and with it, the sad resignation softened. The agonized tension that filled her every muscle drained away, leaving her grateful and sad and empty all at once. He folded his arms across his chest.

"I am a man, Kathleen," he said, his tone quiet and gentle,

"but thank merciful God, now an old one. I was twenty-nine years old when I was assigned to Taos parish, yet even then, I knew this was the grave of my ambitions in the Church. But the death of my dreams of high church office left me exposed to all the raging temptations of the flesh, desires that I had in the fire of my youthful ambition scorned as unworthy of a conquistador of God. Indeed, once here, for many years, those temptations seemed all that were left to me." Father Reynaldo shook his head. His tone was louder, touched with shame and anger.

"Wine, just let me send to Santa Fe. I had all that I wanted. The diocese took my requests as a sign of increased attendance at Mass. None of the Indians here ever dared to ride to the capital and report the white priest who sang drunken songs in the evenings. If the thick, coarse wool of this robe scratched my sensitive patrician skin, why I wore what the Tewa men wore, soft cotton pants and shirts made by their women. And I held a power that could command the women, and their men, to serve me. I was the parish priest, a symbol of both church and state. A word from me, and soldiers would swarm through the pueblo. Yes, the women had to serve me. I give thanks to the blessed Virgin that I resisted that temptation." He sighed and dropped his hands to his lap. His shook his head again.

"But it was not piety that saved me." His tone was lower, less anger now, but more shame. "Many whites say they find Tewa women unattractive, but they lie and know that they lie. Pride keeps their hands off these women, and so it was with me. I was a Spanish nobleman. Honor, the hubris of an aristocrat puffed up with family tradition and heritage, forbade taking any of these peasant Indian women, however attractive, however grace-ful, however desirable. My gentleman's honor told me I must conquer that base desire for the flesh of peons. I was still more nobleman than priest. God had to wait on the years to work on me, break my arrogance, still the pounding in my blood, teach me wisdom. Now, by God's grace, I am more priest than conquistador." He put an arm around her shoulders and hugged her a moment, like a true father. Then he released her and stood up.

"Ah, I ramble like a senile, old man. You have much still to do tonight and a long ride ahead of you in the morning, but I wish you would think of these things I have told you. Think long and hard about Spanish gentlemen. You have never once mentioned James Colter since he rode away." He smiled and held up a hand to keep her silent. "Child, don't shake your head. Your heart was in your eyes whenever he was nearby. Taos is where he, foolish man, deserted you. Now, Colonel Montoya commands the garrison at Santa Fe, a sleepy little capital in a province bereft of gold or the Seven Cities of Cibola, but he is a Spanish nobleman and a soldier. Conquistador honor demands conquest. Remember, you will always be welcome in Taos."

CHAPTER 8

The early morning air was sharp and cool when Kathleen swung her saddle and saddle blanket onto the top rail of the horse stall and leaned her rifle against it. Banshee stamped his feet and thrust his nose at her snuffing for oats, but when she held up bridle and bit, he shook his head and backed against the adobe wall the animal shed shared with the back of the church. He danced and skipped on his unshod hooves. She had to grab his ear to hold him still and force open his mouth for the bit. When she held up the blanket, he twitched and pawed the dirt, but she got it and the saddle on the horse's back and cinched the saddle tight with a shove of her knee in his ribs. She looped her kit and bedroll behind the saddle. Then she hung her powder horn and shot bag each on a shoulder, picked up her rifle, and led Banshee from the stall, but when she went to mount him, he sidled away from her.

"Easy, big fellow, easy." She held tight to the reins. "Yes, we're going for a ride, my painted beauty. A long ride, I promise. You're so eager, I know. Easy, easy now." With reins in one hand and Hawken rifle in the other, she crooned sweet, soft nonsense to calm him. Her daily rides to go shooting in the desert had given her plenty of practice mounting Banshee rifle in hand, and she swung up in the saddle without falling. She nudged his ribs with her heels, and Banshee's high-stepping trot brought a smile to her face.

Ah, he was such a beautiful creature, all brown and white

and tan splotches, dark silky mane and tail, dark-brown, almost black, legs with one flashing white stocking on his left front pastern and fetlock—Father Reynaldo had taught her the name of each part of the horse, how to groom the coat and tail, how to trim the hooves, how to dig a stone out of the tender frog without a kick in return—but Banshee was all hers. Her first horse, first animal of any kind. Oh, growing up, she had called a cat or two hers, but really, they were strays in the Irish slums of Boston, cadging a crust of milk-dipped bread from her when she had one, and when she hadn't any food, which was all too hard to come by, well, they had moved on. But Banshee was hers. No one could tell her this war horse was too much animal for a woman. She had won him—killed to get him—and ridden him across the Staked Plains and half of the Rocky Mountains. She would ride him if she pleased—and how she pleased. None of Father Reynaldo's sidesaddle nonsense. Banshee was a Comanche war horse, and she was no highborn princess. She had had plenty of time to split her skirt up the middle and sew the halves into loose, baggy pant legs. Dress enough when she was walking, but riding pants when she climbed aboard Banshee, and if, when she was riding, a little more of her shin was exposed than folks thought proper, let them gawk and whisper.

There were always whispers enough following a single woman on her own. And men would gawk at a nun covered from head to toe in a black robe and habit. Yes, here, around the corner, all turned out for the day's ride were the lancers, popeyed at her and Banshee. Here was Father Reynaldo, all sad eyes and wistful smile on such a beautiful morning, standing on the church porch to see her off. The man had a school full of children and still looked so forlorn. She hoped a school waited for her in Santa Fe, but with Roger Freepole, sitting his swaybacked grey horse all squinty-eyed and scowling, as her paymaster, how certain could she be? And over there sat Colonel Montoya on a big black gelding—yes, he would have a black with gleaming silver work on its bridle and saddle—reins in his left hand, riding crop dangling from the wrist of the right hand poised on his hip. There he was, all dash and elegance in a blue and white serge uniform and polished boots that flared over the knees. His dark-brown eyes centered on her face, never straying like those of his men and Freepole to the high-riding hems of her skirt. A faint smile flaring his dark mustachios. Oh, what a lovely morning for a ride!

To the east, the Sangre de Cristo Mountains shielded Kathleen and her escorts from the rising sun. They rode southwest following the Rio Taos for ten miles while the thin mountain air out of the east stayed cool for most of the June morning, and Kathleen loved every moment. To the west, the soaring peaks of the San Juan Mountains reflected the golden light of the new day. The night dew had washed yesterday's dust from bright green piñon trees and cacti. Here and there, night-blooming white and yellow flowers, their petals still unfurled in the shade of the mountains, sprinkled the cacti. Kangaroo rats hopped among the sage, searching for last mouthfuls before retiring to their holes to sleep through the day's heat. Once, Kathleen saw a grey kit fox hunting on the far bank of the Taos River where it joined the Rio Grande flowing south toward Santa Fe. Even the bare ground of the desert stood out sharp and brown. This, she knew, was one of the reasons Colter had left her. Towns, even one as tiny as Taos Pueblo, made him feel trapped. He had to be out and roaming free among the deserts and mountains on mornings like these; that she could respect. But on those mornings, they could have ridden together. She would have gone with him, had he asked.

"You are dreaming this morning, Miss O'Dwyer," Colonel

Montoya said in perfect English. Around them, the lancers lolled in their saddles, bored by what must be to them just another long pounding ride in the desert and indifferent to this incomprehensible tongue of their commander. Behind her, Roger Freepole rode well to the rear and a little to one side of the column, out of the dust kicked up by the horses. Montoya swept his eyes across the landscape. "Not that I blame you. In the cramped and dusty barracks of Mexico City, this land of glory is what I dreamed of, too. This is why I requested a transfer. Life in the capital, however rewarding politically to an officer's career, could never compare to the chance to live out my dreams here."

"I wonder," Kathleen said, "what kind of dreams you have, Colonel Montoya. Certainly, the dreams that brought you to the frontier must have broken the hearts of many lovely ladies in Mexico City." There, she had done it—flirted with him—spoken the words easily, too, as if she called to his attention a sudden breeze that died away even as she turned her face to it. Wonder of wonder, he was blushing. A smile touched her lips, and the red deepened on Montoya's face. How delightful! "Come, come now, Colonel. Out here, we have no truck with the modest reserve of civilized society. Plain speaking is the rule on the frontier. Out with it. What wild fanciful dreams have lured you to dusty New Mexico?"

Montoya straightened in the saddle and flashed his white teeth in a smile.

"I must confess I have always been a dreamer tilting at windmills." Montoya swept off his wide-brimmed hat, bowed in the saddle, and then looked straight into Kathleen's eyes. "But all my dreams seem to me now but pale wisps of a callow imagination, for none of them ever hinted at a vision of a prancing charger bearing a rifle-toting beauty with hair the color of flame."

And now, Kathleen felt her own face redden, but although he rode close enough for their knees to brush every once and awhile, Montoya discreetly turned the conversation back to the dazzling landscape. Ah, this one was a charmer indeed, thought Kathleen, never overplaying the moment. By late morning, the sun had risen well above the peaks of the Sangre de Cristo Mountains and with scorching heat put an end to Kathleen and Montoya's delightful banter. Still, he rode alongside her and inquired whether her floppy wide-brimmed hat, the one Colter had given her several weeks ago, provided sufficient protection and offered his own. She smiled and thanked him for his concern but declined the offer. Their party alternated riding and walking their horses for two more hours, taking a ten-minute break every hour in whatever shelter they found from the sun among the mesquite brush. During these breaks, Montoya insisted his men stake up a canvas tent half for shade where Kathleen and he sipped water from their canteens. At noon, when the heat made going on impossible, they halted for a three-hour siesta. Montoya had his men set up the shelter half for Kathleen and formed his men into a loose protective circle around her, facing out while she dozed. In the late afternoon, they set out again, Montoya riding beside Kathleen. They pushed on to San Juan Pueblo, where in the dark of night, Montoya turned the mission priest and his Indian mistress out of their bed to make a cold supper for them and give up their bedroom to Kathleen.

Kathleen drifted off to sleep recalling how Colonel Montoya's dark-brown eyes caught and held the evening starlight, but despite her deep muscle-aching weariness, Kathleen dozed fitfully for most of that night. Images of Colonel Montoya warred with those of Father Reynaldo, and behind them both floated James Colter's cold blue eyes, drifting farther and farther away. When she awoke in the early morning, her eyes were full of tears. She, a grown woman. This was intolerable.

That morning, they set out again before first light, riding along the banks of the Rio Grande, and Colonel Montoya proved just as entertaining as the previous day, describing the royal court at Madrid as an ornate mausoleum entombing the dead glories of Spain while Mexico City with its vibrant political intrigue was the chrysalis of a new empire.

"The Old World is finished." Montoya snapped his fingers in dismissal. "Napoleon was its last gasp of grandeur, but the stinking rabbles of democracy brought him down, like a pack of cowardly wolves nipping at the heels of a regal stag. Now, what is left of Europe? Parliaments of shopkeepers dictating to kings. There is nothing there for a man of vision.

"But such is not the case in North America. Here is the last arena for glory, for empire. Already, the Americans are carving out theirs, but our current president and his mob of democratic cronies act as if Mexico has nothing to fear from the United States. They talk of mutual trade, commerce. They invite the Americans into Mexico as customers, beg them to come, as if she were—forgive me for my uncouth speech, but you bade me speak plainly–a whore to sell her charms to any unwashed peasant with a gold coin. But my mentor, General Santa Ana, is the man of courage that Mexico needs, a leader with a grand vision of Mexico's destiny. He sees the gringos swarming throughout Texas, hears their traitorous murmurs for independence, and sees their grasping fingers already stretching toward New Mexico. It was he who arranged my transfer here to prepare the province for its role in Mexico's glorious new empire."

"But that would mean war." Kathleen stared at Colonel Montoya.

"War, yes. Conquest. Glory." Montoya gazed at mountainous

heights around them. His chest rose and fell with each breath. His eyes were on fire. "No other dreams are worthy of a man." Then he shook his head, laughed, and smiled at Kathleen. "Ah, but now I am the one who is dreaming. Such things will one day come to pass, I'm sure, but they are years away. Perhaps even decades. And the poet says we should live in the moment, enjoying the beauty of what is now at hand."

After ten or twelve miles, the lancers left the Rio Grande, striking southeast across the open desert toward Nambe Pueblo. Away from the river's cooling mists, the sun beat down on them. Soon, a wind blew from the south like the blast of an open oven. Kathleen's perspiration evaporated instantly, leaving an oily film thickened with dust on her exposed neck and face. Thirst was constant, but she had learned from Colter how to fight that off with a pebble in her mouth. Where was he now? High up in a cool mountain glen somewhere, no doubt. Scouting beaver sign for the winter harvest. Hadn't he said that summer pelts were thin and pale, no good for trade? What would he do throughout the long summer? Hunt, travel—perhaps, think of her? Did he ever think of her?

"Colonel Montoya!" called Sergeant Mendoza, a stocky lancer, from the rear of the column and pointed north. "Dust storm."

A wide, long wall of filmy brown climbed into the yellow sky about ten or fifteen miles behind them. It blew straight at them, widening farther to east and west as it came. Kathleen had been through a dust storm at Taos Pueblo, inside the adobe walls of the mission church with its shuttered windows locked tight, and still, the sand had worked its way into every nook and crevice. Unpleasant, a nuisance, but not dangerous. But out here on the open desert, if a strong wind blew, flying sand could scrape flesh from the bone.

"It appears," Montoya said, "we will have a bit of an early siesta. Sergeant Mendoza, break out the tent canvas. Then get everybody down. We'll have to cover ourselves and the horses."

The lancers dismounted and hurriedly unpacked the tent canvas, but wild eyed and neighing, Banshee and the other horses struggled to break free and run from the approaching storm. Each man fought to hold his own kicking and rearing horse. Roger Freepole lost his grip on his reins, and his sway-backed grey took off south at a gallop. Kathleen had to drop her rifle to hang onto Banshee's reins with both hands. She yanked Banshee's head down and seized his left ear with her teeth, twisting her head down and to the left, forcing him to his knees close to her rifle. Keeping a tight grip on the reins with her left hand, she transferred her grip on his ear from her teeth to her right hand. Crooning to him, she twisted his head with the reins and his ear, forcing him down onto his side, despite a glancing rear hoof to her right hip. God, it hurt! But she managed to hold down Banshee, though his eyes were wide and staring. She tugged a rag out of her bedroll and tied it around the horse's eyes, and he lay quiet.

Wisps of flying dust already stung her eyes and exposed flesh. When she looked up, her hat sailed away south with the wind. About a third of the soldiers had lost their mounts, but the remaining two thirds had their own horses down, although Montoya's big black gelding still fought and reared, lifting the colonel off his feet. If they didn't cover the lying horses with canvas within a few moments, raking sand would drive the terrified animals up again, and then the men would never hold any of them. Kathleen screamed at Freepole to help Montoya, but Freepole turned his back to the wind and curled up in a ball on the ground.

Sgt. Mendoza got the other men without horses to seize the sheets of heavy canvas and spread it over the men struggling to hold down their mounts. Then Sergeant Mendoza leaped and grabbed hold of the black gelding's bit. Together, he and Montoya wrestled the horse to the ground beside Banshee and covered both horses and Kathleen with a canvas sheet, each man crawling under the canvas and wrapping a corner under his body. For twenty minutes, Kathleen lay locked with her arms around Banshee's quivering neck, crooning, "Hush, hush. Easy, big fellow. Easy," while Montoya struggled to hold his screaming gelding down. She heard it lash out with back hooves and kick Sergeant Mendoza over and over, who grunted each time the hooves thudded home, but after awhile, all she heard above the howling wind were the thuds of the gelding's hooves.

Finally, the wind died away, and the gelding lay still. Montoya pulled the corner of canvas from under his body and tossed the sheet off him. Still with a tight grip on Banshee's reins and the rag around his eyes, Kathleen worked to her knees and then, pulling Banshee along with her, gathered up her rifle. The rest of the lancers, spitting dust out of their mouths, climbed to their feet with the remaining horses, as well. Montoya knelt beside Sergeant Mendoza and gently rolled the canvas off him. Kathleen asked, "Is he . . . ?"

"He's dead," Montoya said and made the sign of the cross.

CHAPTER 9

Late that night, with Sergeant Mendoza's body slung across Montoya's black gelding, they staggered into Nambe Pueblo. Two more of the horses had broken free during the dust storm and, like the rest of the escaped animals, were never seen again. Riding double had quickly lathered the remaining horses, and so Kathleen and the men had had to march most of the ten miles. Thankfully, after a half mile, Kathleen had found Colter's battered old hat stuck to a cactus, but Montoya and most of his men had trudged hatless through the afternoon under the brutal desert sun. After only an hour's march, Roger Freepole had sat down, claiming faintness and begging for water. Then he had guzzled all of the water in one of the soldier's canteens and demanded to ride the rest of the way, but Montoya had told Freepole either to walk to Nambe or stay where he was and wait for wolves to find him. And so, they had kept going through the afternoon and into the dark of night, until drawn by anguished wails, they saw the square adobe blocks of Nambe Pueblo silhouetted against the night sky.

"Mother of God," said one of the soldiers and crossed himself. "What have we walked into?"

Scattered here and there throughout the dirt streets and doorways of the pueblos, women and crying children huddled beside the corpses of dead husbands and grandfathers, sometimes children. Women gave voice to a keening wail that filled the night while surviving men covered the dead with blankets or sat cross legged on the ground turning blank stares to the lancers' shouted questions. Montoya ordered his men to jerk one of these men to his feet.

"The priest!" Montoya drew his sword. "Where is the priest?"

The Pueblo shrugged and looked away. But when the soldiers roughly shook him, he pointed toward a small adobe building with tendrils of smoke seeping from its windows.

"Bring him along," Montoya cried and strode toward the building. Forging well ahead of his soldiers and Kathleen, he kicked open the door of the church and stepped inside. Before she reached the door, Kathleen heard Montoya swear in gutter Spanish.

When she stepped through the doorway, the stench of burned flesh stung her eyes. She blinked several times to clear her vision, and at the sight of the naked charred corpse of the priest nailed to the far wall, she tightened her grip on her rifle. Smoldering remnants of what appeared to be the altar and its bible formed a black mound at the feet of the dead priest. Montoya turned to the Pueblo Indian whom two soldiers held with his arms twisted behind his back.

"Who did this?" Montoya held the point of his sword to the Pueblo Indian's chest.

"Apaches," the Indian said.

Montoya dropped the point of his sword. "Where did they come from?" The Pueblo blinked at Montoya. Again, the sword point swung up level with the Pueblo's heart. The Indian nodded toward the south. Montoya slid his sword into its scabbard with a ringing clang. "Corporal Ayala, cut the priest down and find a couple of women to prepare the body for burial. See that they wash the body carefully. Then dragoon a couple of these Pueblo men to dig a grave." Montoya smiled at the Indian whose arms were still twisted behind his back. "And see to it that our sullen friend here is one of the gravediggers."

Well before dawn, one of Montoya's troopers knocked on Kathleen's door and informed her the column would leave as soon as she joined them. She rolled up her gear and grabbed her rifle, while wolfing down a handful of corn meal as if she were a mountain man. Outside, Montoya's bleary-eyed men sat a full complement of horses. Judging from several undersized mustangs, Kathleen decided Montoya had commandeered whatever mounts the Apaches had not stolen from the Pueblos. At the sight of Roger Freepole astride a small burro and holding the lead rope to another burro carrying Mendoza's corpse, she allowed herself a chuckle. In the middle of the column, one of the soldiers held the reins to Banshee, saddled and stamping his feet in the chill of early morning. She grabbed the saddle horn with her left hand and swung up into the saddle. At the front of the column, Montoya nodded to Corporal Ayala, who shouted, "At a trot, forward ho!"

The column lurched forward, and Montoya kept the column at a brisk trot for the first mile and a half. Then he ordered everyone to dismount and walk for ten minutes before climbing back in the saddles for another mile and a half trot. By then, the sun was up and the horses slick with lather. Montoya allowed a twenty-minute halt for a breakfast of cold tortillas—then back in the saddle at that now brutal trot. On his big black gelding, he often darted ahead of the column to the crest of a ridge or a hillock, staring at the desert ahead and thumping his riding crop on his knee.

Once, far ahead, he sent Corporal Ayala to bring Kathleen. When she rode up beside Montoya, he pointed southeast with his riding crop toward the foothills of the Sangre de Cristo Mountains. She squinted, methodically working her line of sight across the foothills from left to right, studying each clump of brush or rock, as Colter would have. Shortly, she picked out a lone Indian squatting in the shade of a mesquite clump about six hundred yards away. While he watched them, one of his hands held a rifle upright with its butt resting on the ground. A stray shaft of light through the mesquite glinted off the barrel.

"Yes, I see him." She looked at Montoya, who stared at the Indian. His eyes had a hawk's gleam. "He knows we see him," she said. "That's probably what he wants."

"So he wants to lure us into a trap." Montoya smiled and cracked his riding crop against his leg, making his horse start.

"If he's an Apache," Kathleen said, "maybe."

"Of course, he's an Apache." Montoya studied the Indian. "He's got a rifle."

"That does not mean he's an Apache." Kathleen fought to keep the lecturing schoolteacher out of her tone. "He could be another Pueblo out hunting or trailing the Apaches who raided Nambe. He could be Navajo. But even if he is an Apache, that does not mean he's one of the band who raided Nambe."

Montoya took his eyes off the distant Indian and gazed at Kathleen. She saw the controlled rise and fall of his chest—the tension in his thighs and neck. The hawk's look to his face sharpened. A hunting look searching for an opening. His eyes focused on her Hawken rifle. Most of his men carried lances. Two had old flintlock muskets—useless at more than forty yards. He had a flintlock pistol, but even more out of the question at this range. He eyed the rifle.

"Do you shoot well?"

"Yes, but not over two hundred yards." Her left arm wrapped tighter around the Hawken.

"Then I must beg the loan of your weapon, for an Apache is an Apache, whether this one raided Nambe last night or not." The hawk's gleam in his eyes stared her full in the face. He held out his hand.

"He is more than six hundred yards away." Her right hand gripped the rifle haft. Her thumb slid onto the hammer. "No one, not even Davey Crockett, could hit that Indian at this distance. You would waste a shot from the only rifle we have. And that just might be what he hopes for."

Montoya stared at her a moment longer. Then the hawk's look gave way to a smile, and he bowed slightly in the saddle. "You are as wise as you are beautiful. You should have been born an empress. Warriors would flock to your banner, and I would be the first to bend my knee in service." But he turned his gaze toward the Indian squatting in the shade of the distant mesquite. The gleam shone again in Montoya's eyes. "Please, keep your rifle ready to hand, for we may have need of it yet."

The nearer their party approached Santa Fe, the farther Montoya scouted behind them, crisscrossing their back trail to scour ridges and gullies for signs of Apaches. When his black gelding grew too weary for ranging, he exchanged mounts with a trooper and headed back into the desert until the approaching night made scouting too risky even for Montoya. At the head of the column, he saw to the appearance of his bedraggled command, ordering his men to button up their tunics and dust off their epaulettes. Indeed, he did not speak to Kathleen again until they reached Santa Fe late that evening when with a farewell bow he presented her to Governor Benevedes, who welcomed her to Santa Fe and quickly handed her over to the care of his wife. Then Montoya rushed off with Governor Benevedes to make his report about the Apache raid on Nambe Pueblo.

After a cold-eyed study of Kathleen and her patched homespun rags, with a lingering appraisal of the Hawken rifle, Donna del Flora Benevedes pronounced a few formal words of greeting and, in turn, handed Kathleen over to the care of her household servants. Kathleen never saw the governor's wife again during her stay in the capital. Indeed, by midmorning of the next day, she found herself stowed away by the servant women, with a double armful of clean serviceable clothes, two blankets, and a basket of food slung across Banshee's saddle, beside a squat adobe structure. The women said this was Roger Freepole's schoolhouse, but from the smell of old tobacco and molasses wafting through the open doorway, she surmised this structure had spent most of its life as a warehouse for trade goods coming down the Santa Fe Trail from Missouri. As the women departed, she asked for the loan of a broom, and one of them promised to bring one in a few minutes. With her Hawken leaning against a mud wall just inside the open doorway, she set about unloading Banshee and settling into her new home.

She spent the rest of the morning sweeping the building, arranging one corner of the interior for her personal living area, and planning which of the storage shelves she would turn into her students' benches and work tables. As always, she would need to borrow a hammer and a saw, and of course, she would need three or four pounds of nails. No matter how well employers tried to anticipate a teacher's needs, one always needed a goodly supply of nails to set up a classroom. And a large flat slab of slate for a blackboard. Yes, over there would do—the light from the doorway would fall on that wall. Still, the classroom needed more light, and air, too. She would have to cut a couple of windows for circulation, or none of her students' eyes would ever stay open.

Kathleen sighed. All her primers, her boxes of chalk, her framed squares of slate for each student had been lost in the Comanche raid on the wagon train. She had quite a list of supplies and things to do, but not a scrap of paper on which to write them, nor even a stub of a pencil. She would have to go see Roger Freepole today—oh, tomorrow would do, but it must be no later than tomorrow. She would remind him of his promise to Colonel Montoya if she had to. But tomorrow was time enough for that. Certainly, there were other things to do today.

Banshee needed proper shoes. Yes, she would find the local livery stable, arrange to have Banshee shod and boarded. But she would need money for that, or credit at least. She had none. All she had were Banshee and her rifle, but she would never part with them—never. Nor put them up as collateral for credit. She must see Roger Freepole, and that today.

CHAPTER 10

"As I've told you, we don't need a new school in Santa Fe," Roger Freepole said from behind his office desk. He sat very straight, with the fingers of his right hand resting on the edge of the desktop. An open ledger was spread before him. A jumble of papers lay piled beside the ledger. In the ink well sat a half full bottle, quill pen lying across its glass rim. Facing Freepole, Kathleen stood two feet from the front of the desk. He had not offered her a seat in one of the two straight-backed chairs set against one wall on both sides of an open window, and she had no intention of asking for one. Let him sit on his throne. Let him run his squinty little eyes across her face and body while his fretful little wren of a wife and young son stock the showroom shelves with trade goods just outside his office door. He still had to look up at her.

"Obviously, your late brother, the senior partner in your business as I understand it, had a quite different opinion in this matter, or he would not have hired me." Kathleen took a step nearer the desk. Roger Freepole had to crane his neck to meet her eyes. "I require certain materials to hold school. My own supplies were lost during the journey across the plains, but your brother guaranteed safe passage of both my person and possessions. He also assured me that his business would provide whatever additional supplies were needed in Santa Fe to open and maintain the school. It's in the contract."

Freepole's eyes flashed. "Yes, a contract that I did not sign."

"But that as a partner in your brother's business you are legally obligated to fulfill." Kathleen moved to the edge of the desk, forcing Freepole's neck to crane even further. She folded her arms across her bosom. Had she a ruler, she would have rapped his balding pate. After a moment more of his hateful roaming leer, Freepole pushed his chair back an inch or two with the knuckles of his right hand.

"And you have cultivated an alliance that you think will enforce whatever you say is in this damnable contract." Freepole slammed his right fist on the desktop, bouncing the pen on the ink bottle. "But your Spanish colonel prefers chasing Indians to your skirts. Oh, you weren't aware of that, were you?" Hot, angry blood surged through her face. Anger at Freepole certainly for finding her such an easy mark for his scurrilous venom. And anger at Montoya, too—she had to admit it to herself. "Yes," Freepole said, "Montoya rushed off yesterday at the crack of dawn." Again, not so much as a goodbye and the man was off. But anger at herself most of all. She had known Montoya's attention was nothing more than an amusing diversion, part of the gallant conquistador romance he so loved. Only a girl would have taken it seriously. "Took half the city's garrison." Yet eyes wide open, she had allowed him to dazzle her with his charm, the hawk's look in his eyes, the regal posture, and the slim, muscular physique. "Dashed off on that black-assin horse to hunt Apaches." Smug at seeing through Montoya, as if he were nothing more than a geometric puzzle for her intellect, she had fallen all the more under his emotional spell. Why, she did not even like Montoya but had to admit she found him attractive for many of the same reasons she disliked him. There was nothing tender about the emotions Montoya aroused in her, but only now, she realized how truly powerful those emotions were. And to what she had blinded herself, this hideous little toad Freepole had seen plainly. "And hot damn, I hope he finds them. I reckon he might discover that no one finds Apaches unless they want him to."

"Sir, you are my employer." Her throat was thick with rage. "But you will not address me with such foul imputations nor utter curse words in my hearing."

"I will address you in any manner that I deem fit." Freepole rose from his chair, puffing out his chest. "You may put on whatever airs you like in front of that strutting greaser rooster Montoya." Resting his balled fists on the desktop, Freepole thrust his chin forward. "But nothing he says can make a lady out of a common Irish slut."

Whack! Kathleen backhanded Freepole across the right cheek. His head snapped sideways, exposing his ear, and, with practiced deftness, Kathleen caught his earlobe between her thumb and curled index finger, yanking him off balance as if he were an adolescent pupil who had dared to sass her. He squalled just like one of her pupils, too, and like one of them, tried to grab her hand with his, but she twisted his ear, forcing his face down until his cheek flattened on the desktop.

"You will mind your tongue with me, Roger Freepole. Do you hear?" She gave his ear another wrench.

"*Ahhh, ahhh.* All right. All right. Whatever you say!"

" 'Whatever you say, ma'am!' "

"Whatever you say, ma'am!" Freepole repeated.

"And you will abide by my contract with none of your shilly shallying, Mr. Freepole, won't you?"

"Yes. *Ahhhh!* Yes, ma'am!"

With a final tweak, Kathleen let go of Freepole's ear. He jerked away, wincing and holding his hand to his ear. Kathleen picked up the quill pen and dipped it into the inkwell. Then she picked up a paper from the loose pile, flipped it over and smoothed its edges. She scribbled a list of supplies on it, along with an entry for three months wages.

"Here is what I will need to start. If you do not have all of them among your own goods, obtain them from your fellow merchants or authorize credit for me. You will deliver these items to the schoolhouse tomorrow. Agreed?" She regarded Freepole with a tilt of her head. Face red, mouth open and gasping, he, in turn, glared at her.

"Agreed," he said, rubbing his ear. She turned to leave, but he called out to her. "For all the good they will do you. Set up your schoolhouse, Miss O'Dwyer, and see whether you ever have any students in it!"

She marched out of the office, head high, nodding to the startled face of Freepole's wife, who ran to open the front door for Kathleen.

At midmorning of the next day, an old barefoot Mexican led a small grey donkey hitched to a cart full of lumber, kegs, and a slab of slate to the front entrance of Kathleen's school. When she stepped out of the schoolhouse to greet him, he doffed his battered straw sombrero and, with a wave of the hat at the cart, announced in a soft grave voice the delivery of supplies for Kathleen's schoolhouse. When she thanked him, a gentle smile creased his dark, weathered face. Pulling a leather draw pouch stuffed with gold and silver coins out of his hat, he presented it to her and asked where he should unload the supplies.

Motioning for him to follow, she stepped into her schoolhouse and pointed where she wanted the various materials. Then declining her offer of assistance with the same quiet dignity, he set about hoisting rough cut boards, heavy kegs of nails, and the smooth, dark slab of slate with his thin, calloused hands, carrying them inside the building and setting them down without so much as a clatter. When he finished unloading the cart, he turned with hat in hand to her once more and asked if there was any other service she required of him. She asked him whether he knew all of the American traders with families in Santa Fe, and he told her there were ten such families. She asked if he would inform these families that school would open in three days, and he nodded. When she thanked him, he bowed his head for a moment, then straightened and wished her good fortune with her school. With a soft chirp to the burro, he led it away.

Kathleen stood on the short front porch of the schoolhouse and watched the old man make his solemn barefoot way down the street until he turned a corner and disappeared from sight. And she knew that in Santa Fe she had met at least one true gentleman.

CHAPTER 11

But after two days of sawing lumber and pounding nails, arranging and rearranging the rough benches and tables, framing the large heavy slab of slate, and hanging it as a blackboard, she sat in an empty classroom most of the third day. On the fourth day, she sat until noon. Then she walked the streets of Santa Fe, visiting the trading posts and dry goods stores of the American merchants. She bought an iron bullet mold at one business. A lump of lead at another. Something at each store. After she paid for each purchase, she invited the storekeeper to send his children to her school. Most of the merchants thanked her for the business but said their children were too young for school, or had all the schooling they required, or could not be spared this year from the family business. Two of the merchants ordered her out of their stores, one snatching back his goods and leaving her money untouched on the counter. He said it would be a cold day in hell before his daughters took lessons from a Catholic mick whore. She picked up her money, looked the storekeeper in the eye, and said, "I left my Hawken fifty-four at home. I will not make that mistake again." His eyes widened a trifle. Then she walked home, saddled Banshee, and rode into the desert to blaze away with her rifle at cacti. By the time the sun went down, she could pick out a large, fleshy segment on any cactus the size of a man and knock it off at two hundred and fifty yards.

On the fifth day, she went to mass at the Mission of San

Miguel. After the service, she made confession to the Franciscan priest, a squat Mexican far too portly for a Franciscan, asking forgiveness for the kiss with James Colter but never mentioning Father Reynaldo or Colonel Montoya. Thanking the priest for her penance, she asked whether the mission had a school. He said it did, a fine school serving the governor's children and the children of all the leading Mexican families in Santa Fe, but no, he had no need for another teacher; his three Poor Clare nuns were more than enough.

On the morning of the sixth day, she rode east to the foothills of the Sangre de Cristo Mountains. Rifle cradled across the crook of her left arm, she sat astride Banshee in the shade of a clump of mesquite and looked west toward Santa Fe. Whether she had students or not, she had a place to live at the school at least for a month or two. She had three months wages cash, probably more if she pressured Freepole, but if she gauged the merchant correctly, she would have to call on Montoya for official assistance. She shook her head. That would no doubt pry open Freepole's wallet, but then she would have to shoot one of the Americans in Santa Fe. Half of them already believed she was Montoya's mistress—for God's sake, Kathleen, be honest—his whore. Any further help from Montoya would only convince the other Anglos that Freepole's lies were the truth. She would not abide that word whore from any of them. Yes, she would shoot one or all of them, and she could do it, too. She had killed before—twice. Let them beware of Kathleen O'Dwyer.

She gulped back angry tears. Then she swept her gaze to the north and south and east. The mountains reared behind her a vast purple wall, stretching away without end to the horizons south and north. The desert before her stood out harsh and alive with browns and yellows and dots of green. The West was a land to take her breath away with its hard-edged beauty. The land spoke to Kathleen as no crowded city or plowed farmland in the East ever had. So why did it evoke this urge to violence? She had always been a fighter—had to be. In this world, a woman did not carve out a life for herself alone without fighting. There was always some man wanting to own her—to decide her life for her. First, a father who knew no better than to drink himself to death but, of course, knew far better than she what she should do. And, yes, her brothers, mirror images of the father, laughing at her studies, for larks stealing the books she worked so hard to buy, mocking her precise English free of their Irish brogue, and certain of their right to pick one of their brute chums for her mate and master. Then priests who took note of her talent for languages and math and so wanted to make a nun of her, bind her to the church and men's control. And of course, widower fathers who could not let well enough alone when they hired her to teach their children but were certain what she really wanted was to marry one of them. Oh, she had fought them all, but with her mind. She had out talked them, out shouted them, outwitted them and, when she had to, out ran them. Then she had headed west, and the West had broken something free in her soul—some roaring violent thing that scratched and clawed and struck at the throat, the eyes, or the soft belly just below the ribs.

A little black wasp with a flash of red on its wings to match Kathleen's hair lit on the ground several feet in front of Banshee's hooves. Scurrying here and there on its six legs, it darted to each nook and crevice. Elegant and slender, answering only its own indomitable will, it plunged its head into every hole. Suddenly, a huge brown tarantula struck from its burrow, but the wasp did not fly away. It sprang into the spider's embrace, twisting and rolling, engulfed by the far larger legs of the spider in a frenzied ball. And then it was atop the spider, plunging its stinger again and again into the tarantula's abdomen. Soon, the spider lay still. Without hesitation, the wasp dragged the paralyzed spider down into its own hole. A few moments later, the wasp emerged and flew north into the desert.

With her eyes, Kathleen followed the wasp until its tiny form vanished. Somewhere far to the north was Colter, but that hurt was still too strong to follow. Yet that way also lay Taos, and in Taos was a school with students who would welcome her. What was there in Santa Fe to hold her? Certainly not a school without students. Montoya was just a handsome gallant with polished speech and courtly manners, someone to intrigue a girl with romantic flattery and a boy's daredevil deeds. But Kathleen was a woman. She settled the Hawken more comfortably in the crook of her arm, touched her heels to Banshee's flanks, and rode down to Santa Fe to pack her things.

At first, Roger Freepole agreed that afternoon to her proposal to buy out her contract with another month's wages taken from his stores—ten pounds of lead, five pounds of gunpowder, one pound of percussion caps, a four-pound sack of jerky, tins of salt and coffee, several one-pound cones of brown sugar, a twenty-pound bag of corn meal, an iron skillet, plate, coffee pot, mug and utensils, a bolt of heavy cotton cloth, a large spool of thread, several needles, and a thimble. However, when she insisted on a written agreement spelling out the settlement terms, he glared at her.

"You will not add thief to the names I'm called behind my back," she said. He snatched his pen and scribbled the agreement with his signature below her list of provisions. Settlement in hand, she walked out of his office.

That night, she dreamed she walked among a buffalo herd beneath a prairie sky full of stars. A white calf nursed at the teat of its dark mother. When Kathleen approached, the calf turned into a tall Indian woman dressed in a man's buckskins with a beaded necklace that shone like the stars. The woman stripped off her man's clothes, but beneath them, she wore a woman's dress of soft doeskin. She held out the man's fringed shirt and trousers, and Kathleen took the gift. Then wearing the buckskins, she rode Banshee north into soaring grey-blue mountains whipped by snow and wind. She rode through cold gusts toward faint wailing cries somewhere among those dark peaks. They were cries she knew all too well—the agonized cries of a woman giving birth.

Shivering, she awoke in the early morning dark. Her wool blanket had slipped off in her tossing sleep. Wrapping the blanket around her, she climbed off the pallet of burlap sacks she used for a bed and went outside to light a fire to brew a pot of coffee. The warehouse she had turned into a school did not have a fireplace and chimney. Outdoor cooking—another reason to leave this place. She guessed the time was around four o'clock, so dawn was about two hours away. She aimed to be well on the road, such as it was, north by first light. So drink your cup of coffee, Kathleen, and be quick about it.

Warmed by coffee, she went inside, washed coffee pot and mug, and dressed. Then she laid out her provisions and spare clothes beside her bed, dividing them into groups of related functions. Next, she replenished her shot bag and powder horn and set them beside her rifle, hunting knife, leather water skins, and stained felt hat. Thinking a moment, she wadded a glob of jerky in a clean rag and set it with her rifle. The rest of her supplies she stowed in burlap sacks—making sure to double wrap them tightly for silence—rolled them all together inside her wool blanket, and knotted one end of a long, stout leather thong around each end of the blanket roll.

Then she lashed the knife in its sheath to the calf of her right leg where the baggy leg of her riding skirt concealed it, but within easy reach. Looping shot bag, powder horn, and water

skins around her neck, she bent and hefted the blanket roll—
quite a load, but she slung it across her right shoulder, settled
her Hawken in the crook of her left arm, and stepped through
the doorway. She stood for a moment looking into the schoolhouse at rows of benches and tables, dark slab of the blackboard
on the wall, and her own separate table and stool to one side.
No matter how deftly she had maneuvered Roger Freepole into
outfitting this journey to Taos, she knew it was a retreat.

In the East, whenever her circumstances had turned sour, she
moved on with few regrets. Back there, people bred like flies.
Another teaching position was just a town or two away, and she
never had fooled herself that any position would last more than
a couple years. Maybe, someday, when time's work etched
wrinkles deep into her face, and her body thickened and sagged,
she might find a place where men wanted nothing more of her
than to teach school, but she was young and strong and so must
always be ready to move on. But this move sat wrong in her
craw and, again, she realized this land, the West, had changed
her with its hardness and freedom. The land's vast open
expanses filled her with a sense of vibrancy, of power. She had
always reckoned herself a practical woman, but surviving in this
land taught her to look at the world with the dead level honesty
of a hunting wolf. She had a better gauge of her own strength.

Then her stomach growled its hunger. She closed the door,
dug a mouthful of jerky out of the rag, shoved it in her mouth,
and marched down the street to collect Banshee from the livery
stable.

Out of Santa Fe, she headed northwest across desert toward the
Rio Grande. She pushed Banshee and herself hard during the
morning, rested in good cover during the heat of the afternoon,
and then forged through the cool of night, skulking well out of
sight of Nambe Pueblo to her east and Mexican settlements

along the river valley to the west. Around two in the morning, she led Banshee to the river, let him drink his fill and, even though she had seen no one since leaving Santa Fe, headed into open desert to snatch a couple hours sleep with her rifle cradled across her chest.

At dawn, she wolfed down a handful of jerky and fed Banshee several double handfuls of cornmeal, wishing all the while that she dared light a fire for a pot of coffee. Then she saddled Banshee and headed northeast, in sight of the Rio Grande, but slinking through the scattered desert brush, away she hoped from the eyes of Apaches and other men prowling the river valley. She passed this day on the trail as she had the first, riding and walking hard in the cool morning, dozing through the hot afternoon, and going on in the late afternoon. At sunset, she halted at the branch of the Rio Grande that headed east to San Lorenzo Pueblo until the dark of night concealed her fording the river clinging to Banshee's saddle with her right hand while holding her rifle and powder horn out of the water in her left. Then with soaked clothes and bedroll, but dry rifle and powder, she trekked northeast within earshot of the main river rising toward Taos, still more than a day's ride ahead. As best she could in the dark, she spread a change of clothes across Banshee's back. Several hours later when the clothes felt dry, she watered Banshee at the river and then made camp in the desert, setting out the rest of her supplies to dry in the thin desert air. Changing into her dry clothes, she made Banshee lie down and curled against him for the rest of the night.

At sunrise, still bone tired, she awoke and forced stiff muscles to stir up another cold breakfast—soggy jerky for herself and all of her cornmeal turned to mush for Banshee. She had a good day's ride ahead of her, but if her luck held, she would sleep safe and dry that night in a warm bed at Taos Pueblo. Humming softly, she broke camp and rode northeast.

Like the two previous days, while the sun remained behind the Sangre de Cristo Mountains, she made good speed. Late in the morning, the yellow disk of the sun soared above the tallest peaks, warming her flesh with its tingle. She reined Banshee to a halt and took a long look around her.

There. Something moving? Yes, off to her right and behind her. There, still in the shadows of the mountains. No sombreros or hats of any kind. Indians. Two, no, three of them. About a mile and a half away. All on horseback. Rifles or bows and arrows? Too far to tell, but they had to have weapons of some sort. And they were coming her way. Had they seen her yet?

If she dismounted and hid herself and Banshee among the mesquite and piñon, they might pass her by—if they had not seen her already. But if they had? She touched her heels to Banshee's flanks. Better to keep going, angle toward the river, and see if they followed. If they did, she would have the river protecting one side. They could not surround her totally.

Follow her they did, closing to within three quarters of a mile. She urged Banshee to a trot. For half an hour, they seemed content just to keep pace with her. They were too few for Comanche wandering this far west from the Texas plains. Perhaps, they were Pueblos traveling, as she was, to Taos. If so, she had little to fear. Father Reynaldo had assured her that Tewa were farmers and traders, who would fight to defend what was theirs but respected the lives and property of others. But Apaches, Father Reynaldo had said, lived for war and raiding. Oh, they might come to Taos for trade, but what they traded was the plunder of their raids. If you asked, they told you straight out which Mexican village or hacienda they had looted and whom they had killed, for they never lied. Nor did they ever boast. Lies and boasts were for cowards. So she wondered whether these were Apaches, maybe driving her toward their comrades concealed somewhere along the river bank or dogging her trail waiting for a better opportunity.

Maybe, they were Navajos. What had Father Reynaldo said about Navajos? Not much, except they hated Apaches but spoke the same language.

Again, she looked over her right shoulder. Yes, still just the three of them, paralleling her trail a little to the east about three quarters of a mile behind. Just three horses, no remounts. Might be just a question of who had the better horse. And she had Banshee. If they tried to catch her, well, she bet Banshee could outrun them. Maybe, they aimed to wear her horse down with this brutal trot. Never. It might kill him, but he would hold this pace and more all the way to Taos. If she asked him. No, she could not ask that of him. She would turn and fight first, even . . . even if it meant death or, yes, worse.

Wait! Their leader held up his right hand. Now, they stopped in a cluster, and still the leader held up his hand, waving it palm open at her. She reined in Banshee with the Rio Grande at her back and cocked her rifle's hammer.

The leader walked his horse toward her. The two other Indians edged their mounts forward, also, but several yards behind him and spread out to both sides. All of them wore moccasins that climbed their shins to just below their knees, and their long black hair, held in place by sweatbands knotted around their foreheads, fell nearly to their waists. Each wore a long-sleeved shirt and a breech cloth belted around his hips with a rope, but the leader also wore tan cotton leggings tucked into the tops of his moccasins. While his two followers clutched bows with nocked arrows in their left hands, the leader rested a rifle across his saddle: not a Hawken—probably a fur company trade rifle, much smaller bore than Kathleen's—but a cap and ball, nonetheless. His shirt was light-blue serge, and his flesh was the darkest brown Kathleen had ever seen on an Indian. His broad face had a large hooked nose and deep-set brown eyes whose gaze was keen and steady.

"I am called Juan Diego of the Mimbreno Apaches by the Mexicans," the leader said in nasally accented Spanish. "We mean you no harm."

"What do your own people call you?" she asked.

"What the Chinde` call me is not your concern." Juan Diego pointed at her horse. "This is the favorite warhorse of the Comanche chief Yellow Hand. May I see your hair?"

Easing her right hand off the rifle hammer, Kathleen reached up and lifted her droopy felt hat off her skull, exposing her pinned-up red hair, and then set it back in place. Juan Diego turned in the saddle, looked at the Apache to his left rear, an adult about twenty-five with a scar across one cheek, and said something in his own tongue. This scarred Apache grunted. Juan Diego turned that steady gaze of his on Kathleen, whose right hand slipped around her rifle's action again.

"You are the woman with flaming hair who slew Yellow Hand. His people are my people's worst enemy. I thank you for making him go away. For this reason, we will not harm you. Will you trade for the horse?" Kathleen shook her head. "Your rifle then? No? What does a white woman need with a rifle?"

"The same as you."

Juan Diego sat back and tilted his head, studying Kathleen. He said something over his shoulder that made the other two Mimbrenos chuckle. Then the scarred man said something in return, but the other one, a boy, maybe thirteen, in a bright scarlet shirt, looked as if he had bitten into sour fruit.

"What did he say?" Kathleen asked.

"My cousin says it is too bad you are no longer the teacher at Taos. Then my son could learn more than just Spanish at the mission school there."

"How did you know I taught school at Taos?" Kathleen had never seen an Apache while she was in Taos, and she was more than a little unsettled by how much this Juan Diego knew about her.

"We trade with the Tewa there, and we know everyone who enters Apacheria."

Kathleen looked past Juan Diego at his son. The boy looked at her with the same steady gaze as his father. "How old is your son?"

"He has seen eleven winters."

"He is a big one," Kathleen said. Talking to a parent about his child, she was on familiar ground now. Her hand eased its grip on her rifle's action. "I would have guessed thirteen or fourteen. Does he always wear such bright-red clothes?"

"Ah, Mangas, always." Juan Diego shook his head. "It is his favorite color. When I tell him enemies can see him from miles away, he shrugs and says, 'I don't care.' "

"Well, I like the color red, too." Kathleen smiled at the boy. "Are you really thinking about sending him to school at Taos?"

"Yes." Juan Diego sighed. "He is my son. He will be a leader of our people one day. He needs to learn the tongue and the ways of our enemies, the Mexicans. The priest at Taos is a good man. He would not sell my son to Mexicans. I had hoped that you would be there to teach my son. More whites swarm out of the sunrise every day. He will need to learn your ways, also."

"Do you think the whites are your enemies?"

Juan Diego regarded her a moment and then said, "Maybe."

"Well, I am returning to Taos, and I will be Mangas's teacher." Kathleen looked Juan Diego in the eyes. "I will try to teach him that we are the Chinde''s friends."

CHAPTER 12

At Taos Pueblo, Father Reynaldo helped Kathleen down from Banshee and hugged her close, rifle and all. Then he held her at arm's length for a moment, a smile brightening his countenance with joy. The fear and hunger and exhaustion of the journey slipped from her. Smiling at him but embarrassed by the blush warming her own face, she nodded at the three Apaches. "My escort. Their leader is Juan Diego, a chief of the Mimbreno Chinde`."

The light faded from Father Reynaldo's face, giving way to the familiar lines of worry and resignation. His hands dropped from Kathleen's shoulders. Then he turned to Juan Diego and bowed. "You have come to Taos Pueblo many times in peace to trade, and if you come in peace again, I bid you welcome in God's holy name."

With his rifle across his lap, Juan Diego stared down from his horse at Father Reynaldo. "You have not always welcomed our trade here with the Tewas, whom you call Pueblos. Many times you have told them it is a sin to trade with Apaches."

Father Reynaldo straightened, meeting Juan Diego's stare. "When Apaches come to trade what they have stolen and plundered from other Tewas or Navajos, even other Apaches, or from raiding Mexicans in Sonora and Chihuahua, then I, as God's shepherd, have opposed them."

"It is strange," Juan Diego said, "to hear a Spaniard speak against plunder."

"Although I was born a Spaniard," Father Reynaldo said, "I am first and foremost a sworn servant of Holy Mother Church, and the Church calls it a sin for anyone to trade for stolen goods."

Oh no, Kathleen thought, the conquistador of God, his honor at stake, has thrown his gage in the face of his enemies, even though he has no lance or sword, and they are well armed. But yes, for all of his noble heritage and for all of his many failures, Father Reynaldo would welcome martyrdom. Kathleen laid her hand on his forearm. "Father, Juan Diego comes in peace, not to trade, but to enroll his son Mangas in our school."

Father Reynaldo's eyes widened, and he studied Kathleen and Juan Diego for several moments. Then he cast a scowl at the sullen boy sitting his horse several yards away. Kathleen watched desperate hope and dull, soul-draining duty war in Father Reynaldo's eyes. His eyes closed for a long moment and, when they opened again, duty had driven hope from the field of honor.

"You know," Father Reynaldo said, "he may not bring weapons into my church."

"Agreed."

"I will protect the boy with my life," Father Reynaldo said, "but your people have many enemies among the Pueblos of Taos."

"I trust your word, priest." Juan Diego leaned forward. "But if any harm comes to Mangas, I will paint the walls of Taos with Tewa blood. You had best tell them my words. They know that Juan Diego does not lie." Then he yanked his horse reins to the left and kicked its ribs. Juan Diego and his scar-faced companion galloped south into the desert.

Bitterness etched on his face, Father Reynaldo watched until their dust clouds faded away. When he turned and regarded young Mangas, Kathleen saw that the love of God had little claim on this priest. Duty and honor were his merciless lords. Decades ago, his family had given him to the church. Duty to God and the Church were the measures of his honor, the prison that his family and its glorious heritage bequeathed him. He had kept faith, but where was the crown of glorious victory that duty and honor promised? It was a chimera shimmering forever on the horizon, scorning all his efforts but poisoning his soul with the promise that maybe, just maybe, one more sacrifice would bring glory that would crown him as worthy. And now, in this boy Mangas, with glorious martyrdom there for one more cheap word of defiance, Father Reynaldo had instead shouldered the burden of duty. And his reward—responsibility for the lives of all the people of Taos, a people who wished that he would go away forever. Pity threatened to overwhelm Kathleen, but tears would only scald Father Reynaldo, so she turned away and led Banshee behind the Chapel of St. Jerome to the stable.

In his bright scarlet shirt and sweatband, Mangas towered above the rest of Kathleen's pupils. Although they put on tough faces, even boys three years his senior edged away from him on the bench pew they shared at the back of the class, while younger children darted scared looks over their shoulders at the enemy among them. For his part, Mangas sat with his hands resting on his knees, meeting the other children's furtive glances with that same measuring gaze. From the doorway of the church, while she rang the summoning bell, she watched Mangas. Outnumbered and alone, a boy of just eleven, he showed self-assurance in the set of his shoulders and head, and above all in that calm measuring gaze, not the arrogance that Montoya exuded, but the confidence of a cougar among a herd of long horn cattle. Yes, their horns could hurt him, but only if he were slow or careless.

Yet when she ceased ringing the bell and took her place at

the head of the classroom, she saw a hint of uncertainty in Mangas's eyes, but only when he looked at her. Oh, he tried to hide it with a scowl and stiffening of his spine, but those only served to betray his unease. Fear? He was a male and an apprentice Apache warrior to boot, so of course, he would treat any accusation of fear with contempt, heap scorn on the accuser, and charge headlong to his death if need be to prove he was without fear. Showing fear was what he was most afraid of. Yet when he looked at Kathleen, she saw traces of fear in his eyes. No, fear was too strong a word. Perhaps apprehension or doubt was more appropriate. But why did she provoke this, this nervousness in Mangas?

She was white. But Father Reynaldo was a white man, and Mangas looked at Father Reynaldo with the same predator's gaze with which he watched the Tewa. So what part did race have in this puzzle, if any at all? She would keep her eyes open for signs, but asking the boy was out of the question. That much she knew about Apaches and all men.

As the months slipped through July and August and into September, Mangas sat at his end of the bench for older boys during the day and did all that he was told. His halting Spanish gained vocabulary and grammar. He could write his name and simple brief sentences. He had a quick mind for math, mastering addition and subtraction and moving with ease into his multiplication tables. Indeed, his hand was always the first raised with the answer to a problem in arithmetic.

Answering a question that another child could not, among the Tewa, was rude. Kathleen had grown accustomed to waiting while the faster Tewa children coached the slower ones until they all had the answer. Only then would any of the Tewas raise their hands, but Mangas's hand shot up as soon as he had solved a problem. The younger children squirmed in their seats, and one little girl named Maria sometimes broke into tears, even when it was not a problem assigned to her age group. But on the bench with Mangas, the other boys frowned. For several weeks, whenever class was outside at recess, Kathleen kept a close watch on the older boys, afraid they would seize the opportunity to thrash Mangas for his bad manners. When this did not occur, she asked Father Reynaldo why one night as they sipped mugs of coffee on the church porch.

"Your other students are Pueblos—Tewas. Mangas is an Apache." Father Reynaldo's tone was as fatalistic as Kathleen had ever heard him. "The very word Apache means enemy in Pueblo. Pray God they never fight. For if they did, at least one of them will die."

"But they are just children," Kathleen said.

"Among their own tribes, yes, but not with outsiders."

"I can't accept that." Kathleen slammed her mug down on the porch. "I can't accept that Indian children are fundamentally any different than our own."

"They aren't." Warming to his subject, Father Reynaldo set his mug down. His tone became crisply analytical. Kathleen wrapped her arms around her drawn-up knees. Human nature was the good father's favorite subject. He should have occupied a scholar's chair, Kathleen decided, at one of the great European universities. "In your own country, where all men share 'inalienable rights,' do they mix white and black children together in the same schools? No. The whites would never tolerate it. Just think what would happen if a black student suddenly appeared in a classroom full of whites in, say, Jefferson's own Virginia. Would the black child be accepted? Certainly not. What would happen if he fought with another student? Would it be just another spat between two hot-tempered youths who bloodied each other's noses and were friends afterwards? No, far more blood would be demanded, and not just by the children. The whites would demand the black child's life and the lives of his parents for daring to challenge white dominance. It is the same with Mangas and these Pueblos. Only here, Apaches claim dominance."

"So you do not think the other boys will attack Mangas?"

"Oh no," Father Reynaldo replied. "Their parents know all too well that an Apache like Juan Diego never lies. They will not harm him." Father Reynaldo poured the last dregs of his coffee on the ground. "Nor will they lift a hand to help Mangas or any other Apache when our governor sends troops to destroy his tribe."

CHAPTER 13

Where Mangas slept at night, indeed, where and how he took his meals, and who washed and mended his clothes, Kathleen never discovered. Every morning, before any of the Pueblo children made their yawning way to school, found him squatting at the far outside corner of the chapel waiting for her to unlock the doors. At the end of the day, other children skipped to their homes in either North or South Buildings, but Mangas strode around the east corner of St. Jerome Chapel and vanished into the desert. Bands of Jicarilla Apaches roved the surrounding mountains and deserts. They often came into Taos to trade, and Father Reynaldo smiled on their barter with the Tewas. They were the least warlike of the Apaches, Father Reynaldo said, spending more of their time raising corn near creeks in the foothills or hunting buffalo on the plains east of the mountains than raiding their neighbors. Perhaps, Father Reynaldo suggested, Mangas spent his nights among Jicarilla relatives. When Kathleen asked Mangas if this was so, the boy snorted and said his father did not want him to learn basket weaving.

Kathleen worried about the boy, nonetheless. Towards the end of October, he came to school one morning in fresh knee-high moccasins, pants under his loin clout at Father Reynaldo's insistence, and a new shirt and sweatband of the brightest red hues. Kathleen nicknamed him Coloradas, the red one, and the little children chanted *Mangas Coloradas* at recess in a song about a monster boy who lived in a cave with bats and ate guano and had bad manners. The first time Kathleen heard the song she hushed the children and sent them inside to sit on their benches while the older children played. Then she approached Mangas and apologized, but he shrugged, said he liked the nickname, and thanked her.

But the next morning came, and Mangas was not waiting at the church corner for Kathleen. The little children giggled while they recited their lessons, and at ten o'clock recess, the older boys challenged each other to wrestling matches and footraces. Noon came and still no Mangas, but during afternoon siesta, while children dozed on the floor of the chapel, Kathleen went outside and searched the desert horizon for signs of Mangas. What she saw, instead, was a distant column of thin brown smoke to the northwest. It burned for about twenty minutes and then faded.

That evening, a bugle sounded the approach of a column of fifty Mexican lancers and infantry out of the bright orange sunset. At their front, one hand cocked on his left hip, riding crop dangling from his wrist, rode Colonel Miguel Esteban Alvarro de Montoya. He paraded his command through the narrow plaza that divided North Building from South Building. Men of the pueblo stood in doorways with their women and wide-eyed children peeking around their chests and legs. Many soldiers held aloft their lances or bayonets bedecked with slack-jawed heads, each with a strip of cloth knotted around long, flowing black hair. There were more women's heads than men's, and more children's than adults'. Many of the Tewa men smiled. A few nodded. Standing beside Kathleen, Father Reynaldo asked, "Do you see Mangas among them?"

Kathleen forced herself to study each bobbing head. "No."

"God be praised." Father Reynaldo made the sign of the cross. Colonel Montoya halted the column in front of the chapel.

"Father!" Montoya swept his hat off his head with a flourish.

"I have the honor of beseeching the blessing of Holy Mother Church on our splendid victory over God's enemies."

Eyes narrow, Father Reynaldo stared at Montoya for several moments. Then he surveyed the rest of the soldiers. Many wore bandages awash in blood. Others, teeth clinched in pain, leaned on their companions. At the rear of the column, the corpses of two soldiers hung across the backs of horses. All of the living looked to him. His eyes softened.

"I give thanks for your men's courage and pray for the souls of your fallen." Father Reynaldo crossed himself again. "As I pray for the souls of all the slain." Father Reynaldo shut his eyes and held up both hands. The soldiers bowed their heads; several knelt and folded their hands, but Kathleen, although she bowed her head, watched Montoya out of the corners of her eyes. With a contemptuous frown on his face, he flicked the riding crop against his thigh while the priest chanted a prayer in Latin. When Father Reynaldo finished his prayer, Montoya raised his riding crop into the sky.

"A cheer for our glorious victory over the Apaches!" His men whooped and shook the Apaches' heads. Montoya's black gelding danced sideways, and riding crop in one hand and hat in the other, he swung the horse through a slow circle with his knees, his men yelling their approval. Then he held up his hat for silence.

"Father and Miss O'Dwyer," he said, "most of my men will camp beside the river, but I must impose upon the church for accommodations for my gravely wounded."

"Of course," Father Reynaldo answered. "Bring your wounded inside immediately, and I will send for nurses among the Pueblos to help us tend them."

"Miss O'Dwyer does not mind the intrusion upon her schoolhouse?" Faint smile touching his lips, Montoya looked at Kathleen.

"I will call a holiday tomorrow." She hoped the disgust she felt at the heads of the slaughtered Apaches did not show too plainly on her face.

"You honor my men." Montoya's smile widened, and his eyes lingered on her face. "Would you honor me with your presence at supper?"

"Father Reynaldo will need my help with your men," she said. His eyes looked hard at her, so she quickly added, "But if you will share your supper with us here in the chapel, it is I who would be honored."

"You are too kind," Montoya bowed in the saddle, but his smile was tight-lipped. "Until tonight then. Sergeant! See that the wounded are settled in the church. Then form the men for our march to the river."

At dinner on the front porch of the church, Montoya described how his men had followed a Pima scout who knew where a band of Jicarillas were encamped for their fall corn harvest. Ordering his lancers to muffle their horses' hooves with rags, he had marched his men from San Lorenzo Pueblo at night to within a few hundred yards of the Jicarilla camp.

"I maneuvered my command downwind of their camp," Montoya said. "These Apaches post no guards at night, trusting to their ability to conceal their camps from our eyes. But I did not want one of their dogs picking up our scent and giving alarm in the dark."

Shortly before dawn, Montoya said, he posted his infantry on a rise where they had clear fields of fire into the brush wickiups of the Apaches. Then at first light, he and his lancers struck the camp in a headlong charge.

"We spitted half of the Apache men on our lances as they tried to scramble out of their miserable hovels still rubbing sleep from their eyes." Warming to his story, Montoya set down his plate of beans and corn tortillas. He stood up and thrust his hands left and right as if striking with his sword. "We set fire to the village, and their remaining men fought like wolves trying to cover the retreat of their women and children, but my infantryman shot most of them down as they staggered coughing out of the smoke. Still, some thirty of the women and children, with perhaps three or four men, managed to escape into the foothills. We killed all of the remaining adults. Not one of the men or women tried to surrender! And we captured some six or seven uninjured small children."

Montoya sat down and picked up his plate. He stuffed a fork full of beans in his mouth and chewed for awhile. Kathleen picked at her food, shoving the beans and tortillas around in circles but eating none of them. Father Reynaldo let his plate sit beside him untouched.

"We spent the rest of the morning and part of the afternoon hunting survivors," Montoya said. "Once again, our Pima scout proved most useful ferreting the Apaches out of their holes. His people have been at war with the Apaches since long before Coronado. He could find them where we saw only cacti and sand. I had promised him all of the healthy children and women prisoners as payment, but he wanted only the young children. The adult women and older boys could not be broken, he insisted, but would simply await their opportunity to slit their owners' throats and make off with anything they could carry. Only the young children were fit to be slaves, and he counted on selling all of them in Chihuahua, where Indian children brought top dollar, especially Apache children who were tough and lived many years."

"I thought," Kathleen said, "that our enlightened Mexican government had long ago outlawed slavery."

"Of course, it has." Montoya's tone was full of warmth and solicitude, as if he were explaining complex adult matters to a child. His smile was broad. He put a hand on top of Kathleen's. "But these children are not slaves, properly speaking, but prisoners of war. As such, they must be confined under proper supervision and taught to respect their betters."

"But they are children!" Kathleen glared at Montoya. The feel of the hunting knife in its sheath hung ready against her right calf.

"Yes, yes, they are." Montoya met Kathleen's glare with a knowing smile, then looked at Father Reynaldo and raised one hand in supplication to a fellow man. "But this is war, is it not? Ask the Reverend Father, Kathleen. Children are often held captive in war. It is the way of war."

When she looked at him, Father Reynaldo's expression was at once angry but resigned. He balled his fists together in his lap. "Yes, this often happens in war." The priest's tone was stiff, the words formulaic, as if reciting a chant at vespers. "A soldier may be called upon to do many terrible things in war, but a true gentleman does not boast of his cruelty. He prays to God that he has done his duty and no more."

Middle son, middle son, thought Kathleen, doing your duty as a priest, saying the right words, but wishing that it was yourself at the head of these soldiers. You would not have let your men slaughter women and children, but you still wish that you had led the charge. You would not have lived long as a soldier, and your men would have shaken their heads and called you a fool as they followed you, but they would surely have wept over your corpse as they will never weep for this murdering bastard.

Contemptuous smile curling his mustachios, Montoya nodded his head. "Yes, your grace, these are unpleasant things for a woman's ears, and I have been remiss as a gentleman discussing them in her presence. I will make formal confession to my own priest in Santa Fe." Then he patted Kathleen's hand again.

"Please, fair one, accept my heartfelt apology, and we will talk of other more pleasing matters, yes? How goes your school?"

"I believe I hear one of your men calling for water." Kathleen withdrew her hand. "Please, do not trouble yourself to stand up. I need no more proof that you are, indeed, a gentleman, and I must hurry to prevent one of his comrades giving the poor man a drink of water, for he is gut shot, and, as you well know, it would kill him."

Colonel Montoya bowed once more, but his smile was stiff and tight-lipped.

The next day, Montoya loaded his wounded on carts his men had commandeered from the Pueblos. Kathleen watched while Father Reynaldo walked among the soldiers, blessing them and promising to pray for their souls. At the rear of the column were the Apache children, hands bound behind their backs and roped together at the necks. Father Reynaldo stood with one hand on the head of girl no more than five years old and prayed, but when he knelt to kiss her cheek, she spat in his face. The Pima scout hastened to whip the girl with one end of the rope tether, but Father Reynaldo shoved him away. Then the bugler sounded advance, and Montoya led his victorious troops south toward Santa Fe, with twelve Apache children shuffling along behind their Pima master. The day was mild and clear, with a light breeze freshening the air.

Father Reynaldo came and stood beside Kathleen in the shade of St. Jerome Chapel. "You must forego riding in the desert alone for a while."

"That is for me to decide."

Father Reynaldo sighed. "Those soldiers did not kill all of that Jicarilla band. Survivors are out there hiding in the hills and desert. Montoya's soldiers burned the Jicarillas' crops and slaughtered their livestock. They will be cold and hungry, and they are Apaches. No one is safe outside our walls this winter, not with all the other Jicarilla bands throughout northern New Mexico. The word of this massacre will spread among them, and they will tell their kin and allies among the Mimbrenos, the Mescaleros, the Gilas, the Mogollones and, God save us, the Chiricahuas. In the spring, none of them will plant corn."

"I realize that." Kathleen crossed her arms under her bosom. Another lecture from a man about the safety of women and children. Well, if boys would stop throwing rocks at every hornets' nest, the rest of humanity would need none of their warnings. "But, Father, I have a fast horse and good rifle. I mean to keep in practice with them both."

"Kathleen, listen to me." Fear tightened his voice with unaccustomed resolution. "These are Apaches. They can trail a fox to its den. And God knows, when you start blazing away with that cannon of yours, everyone this side of the mountains knows where you are."

"Banshee can outrun any horse in New Mexico."

Father Reynaldo slammed his right fist against his thigh. "These are Apaches, Kathleen! When they pursue a quarry, if need be, they ride their horses to death. Then they keep going on foot—fifty, sixty, a hundred miles. Whatever it takes. And when they run you down, death would be a blessing you would beg them for."

"As you well know, I have a large-bladed hunting knife." Her face grew hot. She spewed angry words in a torrent. "Its edge is very keen, and I keep it strapped to my right leg. Before any man takes me like that, I'll slit my own throat, and he's welcome to my corpse."

"Kathleen!"

"By all the saints, I swear it."

Pain filled Father Reynaldo's eyes, and he shook his head back and forth. Kathleen felt the heat in her face subside a touch. "And I'll trust to the Blessed Virgin to plead my case to Father, Son, and Holy Ghost."

"At least stay within rifle shot of the pueblo."

"I'll ride where I please."

"Then stay on your horse." Desperation wracked his voice. "If Banshee is any sort of war horse at all, your gun's report will not frighten him, and both you and he need mounted practice, as you have just said."

"All right, Father." The anger drained from her, leaving her tired and a bit ashamed, but only a wee bit. Aye, Father Reynaldo just wanted her to be safe. And aye, she had no mind to rush off like some braggart man to a foolish death. "I'll stay mounted for my target shooting, and not stray too far from Taos."

"One thing more, Kathleen."

"What is it, Father?"

"Take Mangas with you." He held up a hand. "No, hear me out. Mangas is Juan Diego's son. Any Apache that comes across you with that boy will do you no harm—as long as the boy speaks up for you. Would he speak for you?"

"I think so, Father."

"Then take him with you."

"I promise to take him, Father, but first, he has to come back to school."

That afternoon Mangas strode into the church and took his customary seat on the bench with the older boys. At the end of the day, when she dismissed the students, Kathleen told Mangas to stay behind. She asked if all was well with him and his family. He nodded. After a moment, she told him that she had worried about him, afraid the Mexican soldiers had killed him and his family. Mangas's eyes narrowed to slits.

"I am very, very proud of you, Mangas," she said. "And your

father will be proud of you as well when he sees how much you have learned."

Mangas shrugged. "I am a Mimbreno Chinde`, as is my father, Juan Diego. There is not a Mexican alive who could catch and kill us, even if he has a stinking, ass-licking Pima to guide him. I hope you are right about my father. Will you tell him that I have learned much, as he commanded?"

"Of course."

"Good. Then, maybe, my father will say I have learned enough of the white man's ways and send me to serve as an apprentice with my uncle's war parties in the spring."

Chapter 14

So whenever Kathleen rode Banshee into the desert foothills or along the Taos River, the tall Chinde` boy loped on the ground alongside her. She offered to obtain the loan of a horse from a Tewa in North Pueblo who owned several, but Mangas shook his head. When Juan Diego had left him at Taos Pueblo, he had taken his son's horse. His father, Mangas said, did not want him to go soft living among the Tewas and told him to sleep several miles from Taos every night. His father had given him strict instructions to run with his bow, arrows, and the rest of his gear into Taos before dawn every morning, hide his weapons and gear and, in the afternoon, run several miles somewhere else to spend the night. Keeping pace with Banshee, Mangas said, would help improve his wind and make his father proud. And as long as she held Banshee to a trot, the boy stayed right beside her with bow in his hand, a quiver of arrows slung over one shoulder, and a bag with the rest of his gear over the other shoulder. Indeed, at the end of their excursions, Banshee was the one puffing and blowing and sucking air through his open mouth.

Whenever she stopped to shoot her rifle, Mangas moved away about ten yards and squatted on his heels. Their first time out, she noticed Mangas watching her load the Hawken, so she offered to let him fire it. Again, Mangas shook his head. He said he had learned how to shoot a rifle with his scar-faced uncle's Mexican flintlock. Someday, he would have a fine cap and ball rifle like Kathleen's, so he watched only to learn how the Hawken was loaded, but when his father had left him at Taos, he had told Mangas to keep his eyes and hands sharp with his own bow and arrows. Indeed, if a jackrabbit or sidewinder came within bowshot, Mangas needed just one arrow to pin it to the ground. He cleaned the carcasses and dropped them in his bag, and so Kathleen knew what instructions Juan Diego had given his son about sharing the food of strangers.

While fall turned into winter, Kathleen spent many days with Mangas, but she could not say they were friends. He was a Chinde`. His favorite color was red. He obeyed his father in all things. She knew little more about him than what she had learned the first day. Yet she grew ever fonder of him, his quick mind, few words, wary eyes. Oh, yes, she knew that Colter's eyes were blue, not brown, but when Mangas crouched and watched her while she fired with the desert around them and the river in its valley to the west and the mountains to the east, she thought of James Colter. How his eyes, too, had never been still, never lingered—except once!—on her for very long, but restless and searching, always shifted their cold hunter's gaze here and there.

To the north, snow would have long since fallen in the mountains where he trapped beaver. The cold would have thickened and darkened their pelts. She hoped he had found good streams full of beaver, though the work would freeze his hands, chafe them raw, make them bleed. He had ridden north without decent supplies, but he had said beaver tail made a juicy steak. The pelts would keep him warm. If he had found good streams . . . If he was still alive . . . Did he ever think of her?

And when she and Mangas returned to Taos each evening at

sunset, the boy vanished into the twilight without ever a word of goodbye.

By midwinter, Kathleen could hit a target the size of a man at three hundred yards two out of every three shots from astride Banshee, who no longer reared or bucked at the report of her rifle. She was much better at managing Banshee with just her knees, leaving her hands free to reload. Indeed, that winter, her rifle was seldom out of arm's reach. Even in the classroom, she propped it against the wall behind her work desk, despite Father Reynaldo's half-hearted scolding.

Early in the winter, Jicarilla Apaches waylaid lone shepherds and small groups of drovers in the desert foothills and mountains. Dutifully, Father Reynaldo dispatched reports to Santa Fe, but no lancers came to chastise the Apache. Soon, Mimbrenos and Mescaleros bushwhacked trade wagons travel-ing from town to town. By January, Apaches of all bands raided Mexican rancheros the length of the Rio Grande Valley. At strongly fortified haciendas and villages, Apaches contented themselves with running off livestock and murdering vaqueros who dared to chase them, but when a war party caught a hacienda with sleeping defenders, they swarmed over its walls, murdering men and old women, carrying off young women and children. Relatives, if the captives were lucky, bought them back. The unlucky ones, the Apaches kept for their own slaves or sold them north to plains tribes along with horses and other booty. Apaches attacked Nambe, San Juan, San Ildefanso, Tes-uque, and Picuris Pueblos. Kathleen heard wild rumors that Apaches had even besieged Zuni Pueblo in the far Arizona deserts. But without war paint, the Apaches rode into Taos Pueblo to trade their plunder for corn, lead, and gunpowder, and Father Reynaldo dared not turn them away.

But now at last, as winter hovered on the brink of spring,

mounted columns of Mexican soldiers crisscrossed the deserts and mountains around Taos. Often, they commandeered parts of North or South Buildings for their brief stays, rousting inhabitants out of their homes and seizing whatever supplies they needed. But Tewas were skilled at hiding their possessions, and bands of Apaches frequently rode to the outskirts of Taos and slapped their buttocks at the soldiers headed back to Santa Fe.

Brief rains that marked the coming of spring rinsed yellow dust from sage and cacti, and the desert was awash in flowers. Tewas danced their puberty dances in the pueblos, and Apaches held their dances in the arroyos and caverns where they hid their camps. All was at peace for two or three days. Then flowers withered, and spring dust storms stripped the remaining petals from the brush. Merchants dared not move their goods from one village to another without a military escort. More and more often, Kathleen saw columns of soldiers marching afoot.

"Apaches attack only when they have gained an overwhelming advantage," Father Reynaldo said, "so they steal the soldiers' horses."

"Will they sell them to the Ute and Comanche?" Kathleen asked. "Or will they keep them for themselves."

"They will eat most of the horses." Father Reynaldo smiled and shook his head. "Apaches have a fondness for horse and mule flesh. They much prefer it to beef or venison. I half suspect that Colonel Montoya's California gelding made one of the first steaks. As long as you are keeping that rifle inside the church, you might as well stable Banshee in your room at night. It's what the Pueblos are doing now with their own livestock."

Kathleen put her hands on her hips in mock anger. "You just want to get back at me for taking over your bedroom."

"It's time you do some penance for that, yes." Father Reynaldo smiled. He so seldom smiled. Kathleen giggled and

covered her mouth with her hand. Father Reynaldo's face red-
dened, but his smile broadened. "Your horse snores, you know.
Oh, you didn't know. Well, let me tell you, child, of his
monstrously loud snores. Every night, I expect him to draw
Apaches from all over New Mexico." Kathleen shrieked with
laughter. "I thank the Lord every morning that I greet the
sunrise without my throat slit. You'll note I did not say 'wake
every morning,' for your horse makes sure that I get devilishly
little sleep."

"Well, Father." Kathleen wiped tears of laughter out of her
eyes. "Why do you not sleep in one of the church pews?"

"Actually, that's what I usually end up doing." His eyes
sparkled, and yes, his whole face lit up. "But I stay in the shed
long enough for you to fall asleep because I want you to feel at
least some guilt for a long suffering priest. But you're a shame-
less woman, Kathleen O'Dwyer. You don't regret any of the
outrageous things you do."

"No, I do not. All the same, I had best get Banshee inside at
night for awhile." An impish grin spread across her face. "But it
will be your fault, Father, if the high and mighty folks of Santa
Fe hear tell of this. Would they not just love a bit of scandal
about my sleeping with a horse?"

"Kathleen!"

At first, the smell of horseflesh in her room filled her sleep with
bittersweet memories of the journey through the mountains
with Colter nine months ago. Shoveling Banshee's dung out her
room each morning seemed a small price. But soon the stench
got into her clothes and hair and food, a thick choking reek.
Forever on the verge of nausea, she hardly ate and dragged
herself through sleepless nights and red-eyed interminable days.
Then her eyes stopped watering, and her nose unplugged. She
breathed freely again and wolfed down her plate of beans and

tortillas. The horse stink faded into the background, like her waking memories of Colter—there, always there, but plastered over with the rich aroma of morning coffee, the stinging reek of lye soap on the dirt floor, the living smell of a freshly skinned knee on a child. But her sleep, though deep, remained troubled with the stench of buffalo tinged with a thick human female scent and the sounds of a chanting woman intermingled with the birthing wail of a baby.

The dreams, Kathleen decided, were the price for her life at Taos. Here, no one hovered at her shoulder sure that what she really wanted was a man to fill her belly with children until they killed her. Father Reynaldo did not pay her any wages, but she had a place to sleep, food, clothes, a fast horse, and a good rifle. As for money, she had most of her salary from Roger Freepole, and, here, it would last a long time. Indeed, she was probably the richest woman in Taos, but wealth was not something of which she had ever dreamed. For most of her womanhood, a school full of children and all the rest of her life to teach them, those had been her dreams. Now, she had them.

And love? Well, she had had her taste of it. However brief, it was far more than she had ever looked for. All unbidden, it had come into her life. Yes, love had held out a promise of happiness beyond her dreams, and how meager it made those dreams appear, but then it had gone away all of its own, leaving just the memory of its passing. She was a practical woman. She had a very practical dream within her grasp. Beside it, love was just a will-o'-the-wisp, so she was determined to be content, let come Apaches by day and troubling dreams by night.

As a practical woman, she wore the light cotton smocks and skirts of the Tewas and tied her hair in long braids. She put aside her heavy boots, as well, for sandals of braided hemp and leather. For riding, she bought two pairs of woman's moccasins from a Jicarilla Apache woman who had come with her family clan to trade in Taos. The old dress that Kathleen had altered for riding was falling apart, and no amount of patching and mending could save it. Altering one of her Tewa skirts gave her a pair of cotton trousers, but she liked to go exploring off worn trails into brush covered foothills and hidden canyons. Soon, branches and thorns reduced cotton trousers to rags. What she needed were buckskins like Colter's. Good stout leather to protect her legs and arms from thorns and briars, wind and sand, cold and rain. Leather she could use while she rode to strop a knife's edge keen and wipe runny snot from her nose. Oh yes, a pair of buckskin trousers and leather jerkin—fringed, of course—would also be hot and clammy. And yes, they would soon stink, by God, something horrid. But if her nose could grow accustomed to the stench of horseflesh and manure in her own bedroom, she was certain it would not turn up at the smell of her own sweat.

So Kathleen decided to make herself a buckskin outfit—two of them, actually. No wearing the same unwashed suit of leather day after day for her. She may have decided to dress like a man when she rode, but that did not mean she had to live like one. Cleaning the very clothes she wore—or at the least, letting the stinking ones air out—while she wore a fresh set was no trouble at all. Men and their pride. Yes, always talking about their blessed pride men were. Pride made them do this, and pride made them not put up with that. Yet let them get out of the care of women and see how much pride they took in themselves.

Now, of course, she had to obtain a goodly amount of leather, and not just any leather. Cowhide was way too stiff and thick. The same was doubly true for buffalo hide. Cattle and buffalo made good leather for the soles of moccasins, boots, saddles, and harness; but Kathleen needed something much finer grained, lighter weight, and supple. She needed deerskin or something like it. Perhaps, she could buy or trade for the skin of a goat or two, but she disliked spending her money if she could discover a way to get what she needed without it, preferring to hoard her cash for unknown extremities. Besides, with Apache raids, goats and sheep were very scarce, even in Taos. There had to be some cheaper way to obtain that much leather, but how?

Well, Kathleen, think now . . . think. How did Colter and mountain men like him get their buckskins? They went hunting and shot deer. Well, she had a rifle, too. And in Mangas, she had a hunter born and bred.

When she broached the subject to the boy, Mangas puffed out his chest and looked her straight in the eyes. During the winter, he had grown as tall as she was, and someday, Kathleen knew Mangas would be a giant among men. "I will bring you all the deerskins you need."

"Thank you, Mangas." Kathleen picked her words with care, for she knew the boy's Apache pride was still young and touchy, easily offended, even by those he called friends, and hunting was surely a male's role among his people, as it was among hers. "I am sure you could kill all the deer I needed much faster than I will, but hunting is something I need to learn."

"You are a woman. Around the camp, women throw stones at jackrabbits and sage hens for the cooking pot. They don't hunt deer, antelope, and buffalo."

"I am not a Chinde` woman, Mangas, as your father well knows. That is why he sent you to me." The boy stared at Kathleen, but she had watched him turn over problems in his head too many times in the classroom. When his brow was smooth, as it was now, unwrinkled by a hostile squint, his mind was open. "I do not live as other women live, cooking and sewing and bearing children for a man who hunts for me, guards me, and tells me what to do. I decide where I will go and how I will live. If I have to cook or sew, it is for myself alone. If I have to fight, I do it myself. That's how I won my horse. That's how I got my rifle. You have seen me shoot, so you know I can kill a deer if I can get in range. That's what I want you to teach me, the hunting."

Mangas licked his lips. Then he nodded.

CHAPTER 15

Early on Sunday morning, four hours before dawn, tapping on the window shutters of her bedroom snapped Kathleen's eyes wide open. She grasped the hilt of the hunting knife beneath her pillow, pulled it from the sheath, and sat up.

"Who's there?"

"Mangas."

"Ah, good." She relaxed her grip on the knife and wiped her eyes with the knuckles of her other hand. Then she stood up. "I'll be out as soon as I've dressed. Do you want some coffee?"

"No."

"Well, this early in the morning, I need a cup." Kathleen reached for her clothes hanging on a nearby wall peg.

"We must go quickly. Before sunrise." There was that note of worked-at male impatience in Mangas's voice.

"Why?" Kathleen tugged on her moccasins. "Do pronghorn all vanish into thin air come sun up?"

"No." Her young guide had mastered the pitch of the exasperated, but patient, male. "But in daylight, they will see you long before you see them, and then you'll never get within range."

Kathleen chuckled but told herself not to bedevil the boy too much this morning, no matter how much fun it was. Still, she could not resist one last tweak of his male pride.

"But you, of course, if I were not along, could still easily slip up on them?"

"Yes."

"Ah, Mangas." She fought down laughter. "I am very fortunate to have such a skilled hunter to teach me."

"Yes, you are."

After gulping a half-warm cup of coffee while she saddled Banshee, Kathleen rode northeast into the desert with her rifle cradled in the crook of her left arm and with Mangas striding beside her. Even though she had left Father Reynaldo a note explaining why she would not attend sunrise Mass, she knew the priest would worry, same as he did in the afternoons when she went riding.

"You have told me all about where to shoot these pronghorns: the base of the neck, or just behind the shoulder blade, or the center of the chest if it is facing me head on. Now tell me why you have decided to take me hunting for these little pronghorn antelope," Kathleen asked, "instead of one of those big mule deer I have seen up in the mountains. I would get far more hide out of one of them for the buckskins I am wanting."

"We would have to go all the way to the mountains to find them." Mangas had dropped the condescending tone of male superiority. Instead, his voice was tinged with eagerness. His eyes glittered with the light of a three-quarters moon. He puts up with school, Kathleen realized, even does well in it to please his father, but the hunt is where his heart is. This year of living out in the desert by himself is in many ways a big lark to him, a chance to go hunting for lizards and jackrabbits and pronghorns every day, while he dreams of the day when he will be allowed to hunt other men.

"Besides, in the early spring," Mangas said, "mule deer are scrawny from starving through the lean winter."

On the verge of pointing out that all she wanted was the deer's hide, she noted that Mangas studied her intently, waiting to weigh her words in the scale of a Chinde` hunter. She remembered last spring on the Santa Fe Trail how Colter had scowled whenever the teamsters had shot a buffalo just for the flavor of its choice tongue. So she asked, "And the pronghorns will be in better condition?"

"They are smaller than mule deer and need less forage, and they are more skilled at finding food, especially in the desert. They will be much fatter, and their coats in better shape."

"So it is pronghorn then. Do you know a good place to sneak up on them, or are we going to look for their tracks and trail them?"

"Even a Chinde` spends many years learning how to stalk a pronghorn." Mangas flashed one of his rare smiles. He had such a boyish face when he smiled, so unguarded and open. "And I mean you no disrespect, Miss O'Dwyer, but you are not a Chinde`. You say you need a suit of leather clothes now, so I will teach you a way that anyone who can sit still can learn to hunt pronghorns."

"Fair enough," Kathleen said. "But I think you also want to see if your teacher can sit still for as long as her students."

Mangas rewarded her with another of his smiles. Motioning for her to follow, he trotted a little ahead of Banshee. After a couple of miles, the ground angled upward toward mountain foothills, dark irregular humps still quite some distance off. The brush thickened, and the jabs of twigs and thorns against her legs reminded Kathleen why she was out here at this ungodly hour. Then Mangas stopped at the lip of a shallow brush-covered arroyo. Kathleen looked at him.

"We must hide Banshee here." Mangas pointed into the arroyo. "This place will conceal him from passing eyes, and his hooves will drive away any coyotes who catch his scent. Don't worry about him."

"Why do we have to leave him?"

"Pronghorns would see him and stay far out of gunshot range. Their eyes can see very far, like an eagle's, and easily spot the slightest movement."

"Could not I chase them on Banshee?"

"Banshee is a very fast horse, but nothing that lives can run as fast or as far as a pronghorn. They are children of the wind."

"They must be very difficult to hunt." Kathleen slid off Banshee.

"For a lone hunter or two like us, yes," Mangas said, "but when my people hunt pronghorns, we usually do so with our entire band, men and women. We string out in a large circle covering many miles and drive the pronghorns inward. Soon, we have them bunched and simply walk within range. They jump back and forth afraid to break through our circle while we kill all that we need. Pronghorns see very well and run very fast, but they aren't very smart."

She tied Banshee to a mesquite bush. He nickered and nudged her shoulder with his nose. Reaching up and scratching between his ears, she whispered in his ear her promise to return. Then she patted his head one last time and followed Mangas across the arroyo and up its far side. Once out of the arroyo, she turned and looked down for Banshee. Even with the light of a three-quarters moon, all she saw was a dark void marking the arroyo's depression. Satisfied, she raced after Mangas.

They walked for another hour, threading their way around cacti and clumps of sage and mesquite. Once, Mangas knelt and pointed to a pile of fresh dung pellets the size of hens' eggs. Then he showed her a well gnawed clump of sage, stripped clean of its tiny leaves, and pointed to a scattering of pointed hoofprints.

"The herd I saw two days ago is still here," he whispered in her ear. "Look at the prints. See how long they are, much longer than a deer's and wider at the base, even though a pronghorn is much smaller." He glanced at the eastern mountains. "We must find our stand, for the sun will soon be up."

He led the way farther northeast where brush gave way to clumps of grass and scattered prickly pear cacti. Nearby, an owl hooted, and Mangas dropped to the earth. Expecting to see a pronghorn, Kathleen looked around, but none was there. Still, Mangas cowered on the ground, hiding while the owl hooted from what had to be just a few feet away. Kathleen knelt on one knee beside Mangas and put a hand on his arm. He trembled; the face he turned to her was tense and staring.

"What is it?" she whispered. Eyes wide, body shivering, Mangas stared at her. When the owl hooted again, his whole body jerked. "Mangas, what frightens you?" The owl hooted once more, but much farther away to the west. Mangas swallowed.

"The owl. The ghost."

"What? An owl?" The boy nodded, so Kathleen bit her lip to keep from smiling. She had never imagined that Apaches were afraid of anything, but obviously, an owl was some powerful night creature to Mangas. "Why do you fear the owl?" Mangas sat up and listened, but the owl was gone.

"It is a dead soul, lost in the night." The boy's tone was flat, matter of fact, no hint of male braggadocio. "If it finds you, if you see it, it will steal your spirit. You will go away and wander the night forever. We must go on another mile or two to be safe."

"Won't it be dawn before then?"

"What does that matter when we could lose our souls?"

Kathleen saw from the boy's eyes that arguing was no use, so she followed him east while the horizon showed the first glimmer of dawn. As light grew behind distant mountain peaks, Mangas slowed his headlong pace. His eyes no longer were wide with fear, and he looked about him to left and right, searching the desert. Then he halted not far from a large stand of prickly pear cacti five feet tall and heavy with purple fruit.

"See where pronghorn have nibbled at their favorite food."

Mangas's voice was low, barely above a whisper. Kathleen tried to catch his eye with a look that said she understood about the owl, but the boy stared at the ground. "And look, the sand all around us is gouged by their hooves, but their droppings are dry, at least a day old." He pointed downwind toward a rise marked by a knot of sage and tumbleweed some hundred and fifty yards to the northeast. "We will hide over there and hope the herd's sentinel has not already seen us."

They scurried to the rise, hardly more than a swelling of ground some foot or two in height, and lay down among the brush. She gently set her rifle on its side where all she would have to do was lift it a couple inches to fit it to her shoulder, and she made sure the hammer side faced up well out of sandy yellow soil. On her other side, she set her leather water bag ready at hand. Then she glanced at Mangas, but he lay with fists balled under his chin, staring at the cactus stand.

"Mangas?"

"We must not talk. The pronghorn have sharp ears, as well as eyes."

"I don't want to shoot a mother who has a fawn maybe hidden somewhere out of sight."

"None of the does will have dropped their fawns this early in the spring." Still, he watched the cacti, never looking at her.

"I don't want to shoot a doe carrying her fawn."

He turned his head and gave her a withering look. "Then pray to your hanging god for a buck, for all of the does have fawns in their bellies in the spring."

"How will I know a buck from a doe? Will he have bigger horns?" She saw a scowl twisting Mangas's face, but the thought of killing a pregnant doe seemed abominable.

"Bucks and does have all shed last year's horns. Their new ones are now just spikes. Bucks are larger than does. Look for black masks on the faces of the bucks and black streaks on both cheeks. Now be quiet!"

So under the brim of her felt hat, Kathleen watched the prickly pear, and when the glare of the morning sun or dust in the desert breeze burned her eyes, she blinked away water. Every once in a while, she pulled the cork out of the water bag with her teeth and snatched a few sips. Sometimes, after fighting the urge as long as she could, she scratched a maddening itch. But Mangas stayed frozen in place, fists bunched under his chin, eyes blinking once or twice in a half hour. Kathleen watched the backs of her hands slowly redden, even though she tried to keep them tucked under the shade of her hat brim. Then Mangas's eyes narrowed in a squint. Trying not to breathe hard, Kathleen slowly raised her head.

There was one—no, two pronghorns about five hundred yards to the southeast. Then she saw a small herd of them, five of the creatures, drifting in the general direction of the prickly pear stand. They pranced forward a step or two on their long slim legs and, with heads high, stood a moment turning their heads left and right, eyeing all around them. Then one or two dropped their heads to browse on clumps of sage while the others stood guard. Off to one side, the largest one trailed the other four and spent a good deal of time stretching its neck as if sniffing the others who ignored its attentions.

Ah, that one must be a young buck, Kathleen decided. Only a male in the first rush of his budding sexual urges would chase after pregnant females.

By now, they were three hundred yards away and half that distance from the prickly pear. All of their heads were up now, eyeing the stand of cacti and sniffing at its treats, but they advanced more slowly and stood longer on their wand-like limbs studying the stand and the horizons all around them before taking their next mincing steps. Kathleen ever so slowly fitted the rifle stock to her shoulder. The herd came to an abrupt stop with each head turned toward the small rise. Kathleen felt tightness in her throat and lungs. Her face was hot and sweating. She tried to breathe in and out in slow easy breaths. The antelopes eyed the small rise for several more long moments.

Then the big one sniffed at the tail of one of the others, and she lazily kicked at him. She and her sisters trotted toward the prickly pear. They were hardly larger than prairie wolves Kathleen had seen on the Staked Plains. The big one—was that a streak of black on its jowls?—ambled along after the others, stopping to nibble at the ground here and there as if it had no interest in the rest of the herd, and then stretching out its long neck to sniff at them.

The first four pronghorns were now among the stand of prickly pear. Kathleen caught glimpses of white rumps and long necks, but nothing at which she could risk sighting her rifle. The big fellow—it must be a buck, for its shoulders and chest were far more pronounced and its belly thinner—stood at the edge of the cacti, nibbling at the fruit. She inched her rifle up to her right eye and sighted along the dark barrel at the base of the pronghorn's neck. Hold still, she silently told both the antelope and herself. Breathe, Kathleen, breathe. Don't go forgetting everything Colter ever taught you about shooting. Now curl your finger around the trigger. Breathe in and hold it. Squeeze the trigger. Squeeze.

The Hawken kicked against her shoulder and roared, spewing a cloud of smoke that obscured the stand of prickly pear. She heard the patter of thudding hooves and, as the gunsmoke cleared a bit, saw the herd bounding due south across the desert faster than she had ever imagined anything could run. On Banshee, she never would have come within range for a decent shot at those fleet creatures. But how many were there?

Beside her, Mangas grunted. Then he hopped to his feet. "Good shot." He grinned and held out a hand to help her up.

Unsure whether he congratulated her or teased her, she grasped his hand and climbed on unsteady knees to her feet. There beside the stand of prickly pear, lying sprawled with its neck folded back on its flank, was what she hoped was a pronghorn buck.

"Now," Mangas said, "the real work begins."

And work it was, but first, Mangas knelt beside the antelope and, dipping his fingers in its blood, anointed his and Kathleen's cheeks. Then he chanted a prayer in Chinde`. When it was done, he told her that a hunter always thanked the spirit of a kill for giving food and clothing. The soul of the prey would go onto the spirit world and say good things about them to other souls it met there, instead of haunting this world and ruining all of its slayer's future hunts.

Then Mangas showed her how to bleed and field dress the buck . . . and it was a buck, thank heaven. He showed her where the six scent glands of the buck were—a doe had only five—and how to slice them out without spoiling the hide or meat, but he stowed the glands in a small leather pouch. They would squeeze the musk out of these glands and mix it with antelope urine for their next hunt, Mangas insisted, to cover their human odor. Next, he had her break off the forelegs, slit open the stomach cavity, and draw out the entrails. He took the liver and munched on it, saying it was his reward for teaching her how to hunt, and dropped the bladder in the same pouch as the scent glands. Then he told her to bury the entrails. Only a stupid hunter who wanted to draw the noses of enemies, Mangas said, left entrails to stink on the sand. Last, after he had shouldered the antelope carcass, he had her spread sand and dirt over the pool of blood already swarming with flies and ants.

Hot and stinking and smeared with blood and grease, they trudged the miles to the arroyo where they had hidden Banshee, taking turns carrying a hundred odd pounds of pronghorn. By the time they loaded the carcass on Banshee—and he shied away from its corpse until Kathleen wrenched his ear—her head throbbed, and her throat was thick with dust. Mangas had to help her climb aboard her horse, but she was too exhausted for pride to get in her way. After a long hot ride home to Taos, she slid out of the saddle and collapsed on the church front porch.

Father Reynaldo came out with a pitcher of cold water and a rag to wipe her face and hands. While she gulped straight from the lip of the pitcher, he inspected the antelope carcass Mangas lifted off Banshee and set beside her.

"That's a fine buck," Father Reynaldo said. "Quite fat for this early in the spring."

"Thank you," Kathleen said and handed the pitcher to Mangas. "He makes a grand hunting guide. Made sure I learned how to do everything."

"Didn't Mangas tell you that a doe would be much lighter and easier to carry?"

"I wanted a buck."

"And so you have one." His eyes twinkled. "Enjoy your hunt, Kathleen?"

She threw the bloody rag at him. Mangas set the pitcher down and slid a long, thin-bladed skinning knife out of his moccasin. Dully, Kathleen realized she had never thought to look at his moccasins for the outline of a knife. He must have had it every day in her classroom. "Now," he said, "you learn how to skin your kill."

Mangas taught her the greasy process of skinning an antelope and the smelly process of tanning its hide. She went hunting with Mangas many times that spring and learned the whole nasty business well. For, at first, that was what hunting was to her, a chore like boiling fat and mixing it with lye to make soap . . . something that had to be done, and like any other task, the pleasure was found in doing it well. Mangas taught her how to tell an antelope print from a javelina hog's and how to track them and any other creature across sandy desert or stony foothill. So of course, she became well acquainted with the fine points of animal dung . . . what kind of animal had left a pile, its size and sex, what it had eaten, and how long ago it had left the droppings. She learned how to sit smeared with a nauseating concoction of her prey's urine and musk for hours in a blind and not fall asleep or scare away game with a careless move. She learned how to stalk with the wind always in her face, how to step lightly without snapping a twig, and how to pick her way across a piece of terrain so that she blended with ground and vegetation.

She had to kill several antelopes to make two buckskin outfits and learned to leave behind her squeamishness at slaying a doe, for when antelopes dropped their fawns in late May, mothers were forced to hide them in tall grass or brush for several days until the young were strong enough to keep up with the herd. Then a mother pronghorn was tied to the spot where she had hidden her young, and no matter how far she ran or how fast, she always looped in a vast circle around her fawn. Kathleen learned to mark the circle and its center and then seize the fawn so it would bleat its mother into range. "You eat both hen and eggs," Mangas told her, and Kathleen did not argue with his reasoning. She learned that a fawn's meat tasted far sweeter than its dam's, and its hide was softer against her own flesh.

She found pleasure in a good hunt and a clean shot, and she wasted nothing of her kills. The natural world outside of Taos opened wide its secrets, and her classroom seemed much smaller, a place where her children found the joy of discovery but where she ran through well-worn lessons by rote. And at night by candlelight, as she cut and sewed her buckskins, it entered her mind that maybe someday she would leave her students and follow game up into distant mountains where Colter had gone, but then she shook her head to rid herself of idle fancies.

CHAPTER 16

Twice, Kathleen and Mangas saw small Apache war parties skulk by their hunting blinds without detecting them, and once she and Mangas surprised three Apaches leading Banshee from a stand of brush Kathleen had hoped would screen him. She leveled her rifle at them, and although they scowled, they looked hard at red-shirted Mangas, who stood with shoulders thrown back. Then they moved away from her horse and jogged toward the distant mountains.

"Mescaleros," Mangas said, "but they know my father. He has pledged that Taos is safe from all Chinde` raids as long as I am your student."

"If I had fired at them," Kathleen asked, "would they have fired back?"

"Yes, especially if you shot one of them." Mangas smiled. "And you don't miss at that range; that I know."

"Well, then I suppose I'd best mind where I point my rifle."

As frightening as this encounter was, afterwards, Kathleen found comfort in it. Whenever she was out riding or hunting with Mangas, she kept up her vigilance, for one never knew whether Mexican outlaws, Anglo renegades, Comanche, grizzlies, sidewinders, or pumas lay in wait in the canyons and dry creek beds. The desert was home to far more dangers than Apaches, but inside the walls of Taos, she was glad to leave her rifle propped against her bedroom wall once more. Taos felt safe.

145

Still, Kathleen heard accounts of savage Apache raids throughout New Mexico. The Tewas whispered them in the market place, and Jicarillas, Mimbrenos, and Mescaleros who made Taos rich with traded plunder boasted of stolen horses and cattle, of Mexican women raped in their beds, of Pima children with their brains dashed out, and of farmers split in two with their own plows. At Mass each day, Father Reynaldo prayed for the souls of the dead and begged God to fill the hearts of Apaches with mercy. Once, Kathleen asked Mangas if there was anything that could entice Chinde` to show mercy to their enemies, but angry wrinkles furrowed his brow, and his eyes narrowed to slits. Mangas said to a Chinde` mercy was cowardice.

Then one bright summer morning, Kathleen swung wide the church doors for the children's recess and found Colonel Montoya and a squad of five soldiers with fixed bayonets on the front porch of the Church of St. Jerome.

"Good morning, Miss O'Dwyer." Montoya swept off his plumed hat and stretched his right leg in the customary elaborate bow. Behind him, a bedraggled company of infantry and lancers surrounded the chapel. She kicked Montoya in the shin and spun around to her pupils.

"Run, Mangas! Run!"

Leaping clear of the benches, Mangas darted toward the rear of the sanctuary, where Father Reynaldo turned a shocked face from candle holders he polished at the altar. Then a rifle butt to her back knocked Kathleen sprawling to the floor.

"Take him alive!" Montoya cried. "Alive, damn it!"

Heavy boots thudded past her face. Gasping, she clawed up the wall to her knees, but Father Reynaldo already faced the advancing soldiers with his arms held out.

"This is God's house! This is God's house!" The soldiers halted, looking at each other. Behind Father Reynaldo, Mangas pulled a knife out of his moccasin.

"Seize that boy!" Montoya drew his saber and shoved through his men. "Ignore this stupid priest." Father Reynaldo lunged forward, but Montoya with a deft stroke of the side of his blade smote the priest across the skull, sending him crashing into the altar and toppling it. "Go! Seize the boy."

The soldiers charged forward, hemming Mangas against the wall with their bayonets. He beat away their jabbing points with his short knife, but they thrust and slashed at him. His knife hand was soon a fountain of his own blood, and the blade flew out of his grasp to clatter against the far wall. A rifle barrel crashed down on Mangas's head, and he slumped against the wall. With their rifle butts, the soldiers struck him in the face, the shoulders, the back, driving Mangas down.

"Don't kill him, you bastards!" Montoya shouted. "I must have him alive. Alive, Goddamn it!"

Lowering their rifles, the soldiers stepped back. One of them prodded Mangas in the ribs with a bayonet point. The boy twitched.

"He's alive, my colonel," this soldier said and spat on Mangas. "What should we do with the murdering scum?"

"What I've already commanded you, you idiot, to do with him." Montoya waved his sword at the doors of the church. "Tie his hands and get him outside and on a horse. And see that he stays alive. He's no good as a hostage if he's a corpse."

"Sir, his hand is cut pretty badly. He might bleed to death."

"Not if you bind his wrists tightly enough. I don't care if his damn hands rot and fall off. I just want him alive. Now tie his hands and get him on a horse."

One of the soldiers pulled a length of thick hemp rope from his belt, knelt, and bound Mangas's hands behind his back. Then two more soldiers grabbed him under the armpits and hauled him past Tewa children cowering among the pews. Montoya smiled and with a flick of his wrist snapped his saber home in its sheath.

"Oh, what a fine and honorable Spanish nobleman!" Kathleen fought to get her feet under her. "What a proud conquistador you are—making war on children and priests."

Head tilted to one side, he looked at her. For only an instant, the barest trace of a frown marred the perfect composure of his expression. Then with a click of his boot heels and a graceful nod of his head, Montoya extended his left hand to her.

"I'd sooner hold hands with Satan," Kathleen said and struggled to her feet.

"Whatever the lady wishes." Montoya bowed again and then straightened. "War is cruel. I should not expect a lady of delicate sensibilities to understand that a soldier must discharge his too often distasteful duty, but your discomfort distresses me. Though I doubt that Mr. Freepole will share my sentiments." With the back of her hand, Kathleen swiped a dribble of blood from a corner of her mouth. Montoya swept a white handkerchief—doubtless silk—from within his uniform coat and proffered it to her, but instead, she spat a mouthful of blood on the floor. "Yes, Mr. Freepole will be quite pleased with today's business. It was, after all, his business associates among the Pueblos here in Taos who reported that one of your pupils was none other than the son of the notorious Apache chief Juan Diego. Business associates, that's what Mr. Freepole called the Indians who betrayed you, but I shan't sneer. A general must have his spies. I dare say that Mr. Freepole is counting on a sizeable reward from our Excellency the governor to more than defray the wages you extorted. He will be quite pleased, indeed." Montoya twirled the handkerchief around his index finger and tucked it inside his uniform. "But I remain your devoted servant, however ill you use me." Then he strode out of the church.

Kathleen held her head in her hands, but she could not shut

out the terrified sobs of Tewa children but, most of all, the sounds in her mind of the soldiers' rifles thudding on Mangas's head and back. She dropped her hands to her sides and balled them into fists, but she dared not go outside and try to help Mangas right now. The soldiers would no doubt abuse Mangas just to taunt her. She turned to her remaining pupils.

"Hush, hush now. Listen. The soldiers are leaving. There's nothing more to fear." She wiped little Maria's face with her hand but looked at the older boys. "You. Yes, you, Martine, go and shut those doors. And bring me Mangas's knife. You other boys, help me with poor Father Reynaldo."

The boys scrambled to help her lift the unconscious priest off the overturned altar stained with his blood. With her left hand cradling the back of his bloody head, Kathleen sat down on the floor. She sent one of the boys to fetch a bucket of water from the well, another boy to bring clean rags from her room, and had the other boys take charge of the smaller children, dividing them into teams to clean up the church. While the children worked, Kathleen listened to a bugle sounding a jaunty air fade slowly away to the southwest. So Montoya is going to parade his captive, she thought, through all of the Mexican ranches along the river valley. No doubt he is counting on word of his glorious triumph reaching Santa Fe well before he arrives with Mangas.

When the boy returned with the bucket of water, Kathleen set about washing the ugly gash across the priest's left temple. Father Reynaldo groaned and limply pushed away her hands, but she persisted, cleaning red stains from his iron-grey hair and neck. His eyes fluttered open and closed.

"Sleep, good Father," she said and resting his head on her lap, stroked his forehead with a cold wet rag.

"God forgive me." The hints of hope and pride that had long struggled with despair in his eyes were gone. Horror and self-loathing took their place. "I have failed my duty."

"There is nothing for God to forgive," Kathleen said, but the words sounded false to her, for the shame of failure filled her, too, and with it the same despair.

"No, I have failed." Father Reynaldo's right hand clutched the crucifix around his neck, and with a savage yank, he broke its leather necklace and cast it from him. "Now, all of these people will pay for my weakness, my failings."

"Surely, Juan Diego won't dare attack us while Montoya holds his son hostage."

Father Reynaldo rocked his head back and forth in Kathleen's lap. "Juan Diego is an Apache. When he learns of this, he may simply decide his son is already gone beyond hope of recovery. Or he may offer ransom for Mangas's safe return, but he will never break his vow to slaughter everyone in Taos. Will our Colonel Montoya or the governor care when Juan Diego descends with fire and blade on miserable little Taos at the far end of the province? What's a few more stinking disloyal Indians massacred by their own kind next to a splendid victory to cry through the streets of Mexico City? Both men will certainly receive medals. Why they may even win recall to the capital itself!"

"We must get the Tewas to flee to Santa Fe," Kathleen said. "It has a large garrison. Not even Juan Diego dares attack it directly."

But the priest just shook his head. "This is their home from time immemorial. Oh, a few of them may run away and hide in Santa Fe or another pueblo, but the vast majority will stay. Some will fight. Many will just stand there staring at knives in the hands that cut their hearts out, but all will die. Juan Diego has sworn, and he is a man of his word. I cannot leave them, even though I am not worthy to mingle my blood with theirs, but I am their priest."

"No, no." Now, it was Kathleen who shook her head. A light flared in Father Reynaldo's eyes.

"But you could flee from here." Again, she shook her head *no*. "Yes, gather as many children as you can and flee to the capital." *No.* "Montoya and the governor will be honor bound to take you in." *No, no, no.* Father Reynaldo clutched her arm. "You must do it. You must."

She jerked her arm free of his fingers. Rage shook her. A hunter she had dared call herself, yet she had let herself be stalked and treed without so much as a shot fired. And Father Reynaldo, a priest shamed by his own never ending failures, yet willing, nay eager, to share martyrdom with a people who hated him. Yes, send the woman Kathleen away to safety, one last grand bow before the altar of duty. But would the memory of his last noble gesture comfort him when his eyes beheld the Tewa butchered in this very church, when their death shrieks filled his dying ears? No. He would die ashamed, without any hope of redemption. The rage drained from her. She saw what she must do. When the parents of her students came seeking their children, she told them to take good care of Father Reynaldo, kissed his forehead, and went to her room to collect her gear.

Stripping off her blouse and skirt, she tugged on a finished leather jersey and trousers. Next, she belted her knife in its sheath around her waist and pulled on a pair of Apache moccasins, slipping Mangas's knife into one of them. Checking the levels of her powder horn and shot bag, she looped them around her neck, stooped, and slung her saddle, blanket, and bridle over one shoulder, then stood up and grabbed her hat and rifle. She would load in the saddle. Kicking the door shut behind her, she headed to the animal pen to collect Banshee.

Montoya would march quickly to the first hacienda on the Rio Grande, she decided, but once there, he would enjoy the acclaim and hospitality of its owner. He would spend each night at a different ranch, showing off his prize, turning the march along the river into a Roman triumph. She might sneak into one of the haciendas and try to free Mangas, but Montoya would keep the boy close at hand and well guarded to impress his hosts and no doubt their wives and daughters. More likely, she would have to surprise Montoya somewhere on the march, when his yawning soldiers shuffled along with their heads aching with liquor and pole'. Somewhere, she could first catch Mangas's eye and hope he was not too dazed from abuse and so understood her signal. Somewhere she could ride through a company of armed soldiers, cut Mangas free, and ride out again. But where and when? And, more importantly, how? It was a fool's plan, but all she had.

CHAPTER 17

On swift-footed Banshee, she caught sight of the dust kicked up by the plodding column miles before the soldiers reached the Rio Grande, so she circled around in front of them. She found a little hill a couple hundred yards off Montoya's line of march and tied Banshee out of sight on the far side. Then with the sun directly behind her, she lay down at the crest of the hill to watch the troops go past.

First, came a vanguard of four lancers three hundred yards ahead of the main body. Although this advance guard was mounted, only one of the lancers rode a horse—a rather gaunt swaybacked grey nag that put Kathleen in mind of Don Quixote's broken down plow horse charger. Two of the men rode a pair of matched red-brown mules, most likely some teamster's commandeered draft animals. Boots almost touching the ground, the fourth lancer, who wore a look of clinched-jawed disgust, sat astride a large burro.

At the head of the main column rode Montoya and another officer. Montoya's horse was a large-boned bay—Father Reynaldo must have been right about the black gelding—serviceable but with none of the elegant black's fire. The other officer's mount looked decent enough, if thin and splay-footed. Behind the officers, a sergeant had a lead rope tied to his saddle and looped around the neck of Mangas trudging several yards behind him. Apparently, Montoya had thought better of allowing an Apache to ride, even with bound hands. Yes, Montoya meant to keep his prisoner close at hand. Even with his hands tied behind his back, the boy's head was up, and he did not limp. Kathleen had worried that Mangas would be too injured to help, but she had also counted on his being mounted. She sighed. Somehow, she had to get him on horseback.

Behind Montoya's sergeant, the common soldiers walked or rode, but no one paid much attention to military units or formations. Infantry walked alongside less numerous cavalry, and many lancers had to walk, too. Those fortunate enough to have horses or mules rode sway-backed, half-starved animals that surely no amount of spurring and whipping could goad to more than a trot, much less a charge. Few of the lancers still wore their glittering brass hussar helmets or dapper, short-rimmed, black velvet sombreros. Most, like their brother infantry, wore the battered, wide-rimmed, straw headgear of peasants, and a goodly number went bare headed.

Of the more numerous foot soldiers, not one had a complete uniform. Most wore sandals, and about a third were barefoot. The majority still carried flintlock muskets, but quite a few had nothing more than machetes or sharpened poles, like the lancers. Bringing up the rear of the column, now that they were no longer needed, and off a little to the upwind side to escape the main body's dust trudged native scouts—by the look of them, Pimas from Sonorra, but a couple of Navajos, too, probably dragooned for their knowledge of the local terrain.

All in all, Montoya's command was a dirty ragamuffin assortment, looking more like a gang of bandits than soldiers. At least that was in her favor. Still, there were close to fifty of them, all armed more or less. All eager to get their hostage to Santa Fe. Damn it, Kathleen, dog their line of march, pick a likely spot, and go for the boy but stop reckoning odds you already know. Unless of course, you decide to go back and wait to die with the good father at Taos Pueblo.

After the column passed her little hill, she slipped over its crest to untie Banshee and scout the way ahead.

Each night of the march, the soldiers bivouacked at a different ranchero, and Montoya and his executive officer were honored guests inside the thick walls of each hacienda. Camped without a fire in some hidden arroyo or dense stand of mesquite, Kathleen listened to their nightly celebrations. When music and laughter finally subsided, she crept as near the sentries as she dared to look for Mangas, but she never saw him. The third night, knife in hand, she crawled past dozing pickets and slunk through the sleeping encampment to within thirty yards of the hacienda. She circled the house, but at each doorway stood a pair of guards. Every half hour, a corporal stepped out of the house to check them, so she slipped once more past sentries on the edge of the encampment and snatched an hour or so of sleep.

Dawn found her skulking along the banks of the Rio Grande well before Montoya's bugler sounded reveille. She bypassed dozens of places where she could take a stand and pick off two, maybe three, soldiers before the rest would spot telltale grey smoke from her Hawken and force her to flee. Given the plight of Montoya's cavalry, she was quite confident Banshee could outrun them all, even Pimas and Navajos. But what good would that do Mangas bound as he was? Think, Kathleen, think! You're a teacher. Study the problem, and find a solution.

Before anything else, she had to get Mangas's hands free. If he could then somehow get on a horse, maybe, just maybe, she could panic the soldiers long enough for him to break free. Once Mangas was clear of the main column, the Mexican infantry would be useless, but Montoya was not some witless coward. He would lead every mounted soldier he had after Mangas as fast as they could ride. That meant she would have to ride and shoot at the same time to cover Mangas. If she could hit enough of them, if somehow they thought a large war party of Apaches were attacking them, if, if, if. Well, it was all she could see to do.

But how to free Mangas's hands?

Get him a knife somehow. Now, she knew what to look for—ah, her grammar was shot to hell, but so was everything else—someplace she could stash his knife where Mangas, but not the soldiers, would see it. How he would pick it up and cut his bonds without alerting the soldiers, she had no idea. Here, next to the trail along the river bank was a likely place, a patch of yellow grass at the base of a juniper sapling. She climbed off Banshee and pulled Mangas's knife out of her moccasin. She stuck the blade in the ground right against the bark of the juniper sapling. Just the yellow-stained bone handle wrapped in brown leather showed. She poured a little dust on the knife hilt. There, only someone looking for it would see the handle. She swung back up in the saddle. Now, she had to pick a proper blind.

She rode east, away from the river, selecting a narrow wash two feet or so deep and about two hundred and fifty yards away from the trail. Scattered clumps of sagebrush screened the wash. She would have preferred a stand of cacti some fifty yards farther on, but she had to be close enough to be certain she could knock that sergeant with the lead rope out of his saddle without injury to his horse. Yes, in this wash, she could sit astride Banshee with just her head and shoulders showing above the brush. With the sun at her back, she might kill three or four of them before they figured out where she hid.

She rode north three miles toward the ranchero where Montoya had spent last night. The soldiers should be breaking camp right about now. She had to find a place where she could tip off Mangas to her plans without anyone else spotting her. This time she left Banshee concealed about four hundred yards from the trail. Then she hurried forward some three hundred and fifty yards to a clump of three prickly pear, whose fruit had long since fallen off and withered to dry brown husks in the summer heat. Working her way into the middle of the cacti—thank God for her stout leather buckskins—she crouched on her knees and stared at the trail. She did not fear the Mexican soldiers, for lulled by the calm of the last four days, their eyes would be full of sleep and bloodshot from drink, but she prayed for a morning wind to blow from the northwest to swirl the column's dust in her direction and keep the Pimas and Navajos on the far side of the trail.

About nine o'clock, the advance guard of the column ambled by her hideout, nodding in their saddles. Then Montoya rode by, one hand cocked on his hip. His regal head was up, but his eyes, though clear and unblinking, focused ahead on the distant horizon where surely those eyes envisioned capital throngs preparing a festival in his honor. Close behind him came his second-in-command, with the sergeant leading Mangas at the end of that rope. The boy's head was down, watching for nothing save the next step in his path. Just before he reached a point directly between her and the river, she hooted like an owl.

The soldiers trudged on, but Mangas's head shot up, his eyes bright and searching the desert to his east. She slid her own knife out of its sheath and held it above the tops of the prickly pear. Then she hooted again. Mangas's eyes riveted on the knife. She pulled it down and, rising a little, took off her hat and let the sunlight catch fire in her hair. The boy nodded and looked away. She ducked out of sight. Good. A long way to go and a devil of a chance to get there, but she and Mangas were on their way together.

As soon as the column passed, she ran to where she had concealed Banshee and galloped hard south. She counted on the sun in the east to keep the soldiers and their scouts' eyes off the dust wisps kicked up by Banshee's flying hooves. She circled around and came into the little wash straight from the east. Lather darkened Banshee's mane and coat, but by the time the vanguard approached, he had stopped panting and stood rock still with his ears pricked up.

"You know, do you not, my bonny war horse?" she whispered. "It is time for battle, brave one. Make me proud."

Next, Montoya, his eyes still full of dreams of glory, rode past the juniper sapling. Then his officer passed by, almost trampling it. Last came the sergeant leading Mangas. Kathleen drew a bead on his left shoulder. When Mangas was a step away from the sapling, he seemed to stumble and then fell to his knees. The sergeant's horse lurched forward a step, and Mangas rolled across the sapling, arching his back and digging in his feet. The sergeant spurred his horse, yanking Mangas to his knees. The boy stood up and shuffled forward, so the sergeant reined back his horse and again slouched in the saddle. Mangas followed along for another three steps. Then gripping his knife, he threw both freed arms straight above his head. Kathleen squeezed the trigger.

She heard Mangas let loose a hoarse, warbling cry, and she screamed her best imitation of a Comanche war howl in return. Soldiers' frightened shouts and curses filled the air. When her gunsmoke cleared, she saw Mangas astride the dead sergeant's horse and kicking its flanks. He galloped straight past Montoya, hamstringing the Spaniard's bay with his knife as he flew by. Screaming, Montoya's horse went down in a heap of thrashing hooves. Kathleen poured a three count of powder in the barrel of her rifle and rammed a patch home with the rod. Mounted lancers struggled to stay on frightened mounts bucking this way and that. Kathleen dropped a heavy lead ball in the barrel and tamped it down. Foot soldiers fired at Mangas, bringing fierce curses from Montoya and his second-in-command, who had pulled Montoya clear of his downed animal. Kathleen tapped a percussion cap in place on the rifle anvil. Other soldiers fired blind volleys at the desert. Montoya was hidden from her sight by his fellow officer and his horse. She aimed at the man's horse, and her shot sent horse and rider tumbling head over heels. She howled another yipping war cry. Many panicked soldiers threw their weapons away and ran toward the river, but Montoya yanked a lancer off his saddle and leaped aboard the horse.

Where was Mangas? Sweet Jesus, save us. He was headed for the river.

She poured another measure of powder in her Hawken, tapped down the patch, and kicked Banshee into a dead run. But when she tried to fit a ball into the barrel, the lead dropped to the ground. Ramrod still clenched between her teeth, she thundered right past wild-eyed soldiers scattering in all directions.

Ahead some hundred yards at the river bank, Montoya, with drawn saber, chased Mangas, who wove his slower mount right and left dodging the slashing blade. Sandy mud spun from their horses' hooves. Both animals struggled hock deep in river muck. Lashing Banshee's rump with the reins, Kathleen closed fast on Montoya, now fifty yards away, but Montoya rammed his mount chest first against Mangas's smaller chestnut, dumping both horse and Mangas in the shallow water. Montoya slashed down at Mangas, who ducked the blade and dove into deeper water with Montoya urging his horse after the boy. Twenty yards behind, Kathleen and Banshee hit the river at a full gallop, water spraying out like wings.

Montoya, face hideous with rage, forced his horse deeper and deeper into the river, hacking and slashing at Mangas's head whenever the boy came up for air. Montoya's gone mad,

Kathleen thought. He's doesn't care about a hostage anymore. He's going to kill the boy.

Banshee had to swim, but Montoya was just five yards away. Now two. Montoya stood in the stirrups, right arm flung back for a killing stroke. Kathleen was just a yard away. Mangas's head popped up beside Montoya's horse. Down flashed the saber. Mangas dodged, but a sickening *thwack* marked the blade's impact, blood staining the river. Montoya wrenched his saber out of Mangas's left shoulder for another stroke.

Grabbing her rifle with both hands, Kathleen swung with all her might, striking Montoya flat in the middle of his spine with the steel barrel. His upper body slammed forward across the neck of his bay, and his saber twirled from his outflung hand. Mouth gaping, he twisted his head around just in time to receive another blow across his face. Arms and neck limp, he slid off his horse and disappeared beneath the dark-green river. Kathleen tore the ramrod out of her teeth.

"Mangas! Mangas!"

The boy drifted away from her in the current, clutching at the red canyon in his shoulder and kicking feebly to stay afloat. She urged Banshee past the other horse, which nosed around and headed back for shore. Bullets cracked over her head, and two balls kicked up geysers in the water several feet away. She glanced over her shoulder at a growing body of Mexican soldiers, some running along the river bank while others knelt and aimed their weapons. Thank God, Kathleen thought, all they've got are muskets. If I can just catch hold of Mangas and drag him a little farther out in the river, they'll never hit us with those smoothbores.

Sobbing for air, she reached out and snagged hold of Mangas by the hair, pulling him to Banshee and turning the horse's head toward the far shore. Picking up speed in the main river current, she wrapped one arm around Mangas and clung to her saddle horn while she clutched her rifle with her other hand. Soon, though soldiers ran along the river shooting and cursing, she left them way behind. Several hundred yards downstream, Banshee touched ground and scrambled up the bank. Kathleen helped Mangas out of sight of the river into the shade of a boulder and tore his shirt into long strips to bind his shoulder.

"Whatever did you run to the river for?" The gash in his shoulder was deep, but the knobby bone of his shoulder, although broken, had protected the artery beneath it. She lashed the bindings tight, but whether dulled by shock or stubborn Apache courage, Mangas merely looked at her.

"All the time I was walking behind that horse, I was thinking about the river." A thin smile flitted across his lips. "Every Apache warrior learns to swim, and I was always the best swimmer of all the boys in my tribe. I was sure if I could reach the river they couldn't catch me."

Kathleen knotted the last of the bindings and muttered, "The best laid plans, or should I say hare-brained schemes?"

"What?"

"Nothing."

With Mangas riding Banshee, Kathleen traveled north staying west of the river. She kept a sharp eye open for the Pima and Navajo scouts, but with Montoya and his second-in-command dead, she reckoned the survivors would head to Santa Fe as fast as they could march. No doubt, by the time they reached the capital, whoever assumed command would tell a tale of heroic battle with five hundred, no, a thousand blood thirsty Apaches led by none other than ruthless Juan Diego himself. But the truth was bound to come out, and then nowhere in New Mexico would she be safe, especially in the little school at Taos Pueblo. Once she had safely returned Mangas to his Mimbrenos, she would have to pack her kit and leave.

To her surprise, she discovered that she was eager to put New Mexico behind her. Oh, to be sure, this ancient land of scorched deserts, brown wind-swept foothills, and distant knife-edged mountains possessed a harsh, enthralling beauty, but the land held too many peoples, each hating their neighbors and nurturing age-old feuds with fresh blood. As Montoya had foreseen, her own countrymen, while just a handful now, were set to swarm through the province like locusts, bringing their hates, their feuds, their greeds and lusts to add to the mix. So to hell with all of them.

They journeyed north for two days before crossing the river. Each evening, after they had set up camp out of sight of any passersby, Kathleen stalked game that came down to the river for a drink, a gamey jackrabbit for dinner the first night, a rank water rat the second. They roasted both over tiny fires that Mangas showed her how to build in fire pits wide enough to let in plenty of air but deep enough to conceal the flames, and he showed her which woods burned with little smoke. On the second day, Mangas insisted on taking turns walking and riding. Never did Kathleen see him wince in pain. His wound seemed no more to him than a piece of clothing he wore for show. His eyes were keen with their predator's gaze—alert to see and strike. Time to cut the jesses, Kathleen decided. Oh, in a better world, Kathleen would have striven to nurture Mangas's talent for mathematics, for he had the makings of a fine engineer. Perhaps, she could have turned that hawk's gaze to building bridges or soaring buildings, but in this world, Mangas would be a Mimbreno Apache warrior. Maybe someday a great chief. The boy had enough of the white man's school to serve his people's needs.

After they swam the river on the morning of the third day, they paused a while on the far side to dry their clothes and powder. Mangas gathered greasy mesquite boughs and green sagebrush for a signal fire. His father, Mangas said, was sure to have heard by now of his capture by the Mexicans. Juan Diego had to be told of Mangas's escape before the Apache chief unleashed his warriors on Taos. When the fire was lit, Mangas used Banshee's saddle blanket to send up smoke signals.

"Will they see it, do you think?" Kathleen asked.

"Someone among my people," Mangas said, "is always watching. My father will soon know."

Late the next afternoon, within sight of Taos Pueblo, Mangas stopped in mid-stride and grabbed hold of Banshee's bit. Then Juan Diego, his scar-faced cousin, and twenty other Apache warriors rose up from their hiding places a hundred yards up the trail. Although she cocked her rifle hammer, she let the Hawken rest in the crook of her left arm. Mangas looked at her and grinned.

"You would make a great Chinde` warrior."

"But I'm a woman."

Mangas shrugged and faced his approaching tribesmen. They halted in a semi-circle some twenty yards around her and Mangas, except for Juan Diego and his cousin, who advanced and looked the boy up and down. The scar-faced cousin poked Mangas's wounded shoulder and grunted something to Juan Diego, who laughed. Then father embraced his son, who suddenly was all awkward teenage boy trying to stand tall and stiff backed and, at the same time, cling to his father with his good arm. Arm around his son, Juan Diego looked at Kathleen.

"You said you would teach my son that not all white men are the Chinde`'s enemies. You did not lie. That is very strange for a white."

"Father Reynaldo and the Tewas are safe?" Kathleen asked.

"I am a Chinde`. I do not lie." Juan Diego waved at the western sky. "We saw the smoke message and spared your friend the priest and the Tewas, even though they betrayed us to the Mexicans."

"Thank you." There was an awkward silence while Kathleen waited, uncertain what the Mimbrenos would do now.

"Miss O'Dwyer killed the Mexican leader who captured me." Mangas's voice was loud, cracking with high-pitched notes. "She ambushed the whole column by herself and freed me."

Juan Diego stared hard at Kathleen. His eyes looked over Banshee and the Hawken cradled in her left arm, lingering a moment on the cocked hammer and her right finger circling the trigger. He grunted, and his warriors rested their own rifle butts on the ground. Scar-face said something that made Juan Diego smile.

"I must be getting along now," Kathleen said.

"You cannot stay with the Tewa in Taos," Juan Diego said. "The Mexicans will come there and kill you."

"I know, but I have to collect my things before I go."

"Where will you go?"

"I am not sure, but I reckon any place will do as long as it is not New Mexico."

"My people would be proud to take you in." Juan Diego looked at his scar-faced cousin. "One of my warriors would surely take you as his wife and protect you."

"And take my rifle, too, of course?"

"Of course," Juan Diego said. Beside him, Mangas smiled.

"And I would cook his meals and bear his children?" His shoulders quivering, Mangas clamped a hand to his mouth. Juan Diego's eyebrows shot up.

"Yes."

"And when he drank too much of that foul corn Tizwin your people brew"—a smile touching the corners of her lips, Kathleen looked at Mangas—"would he beat me to make me a better wife?"

"Yes."

Mangas doubled over laughing. The other Chinde`s eyed Mangas and then exchanged amused looks.

"Thank you, no. You are going to need all the warriors you have . . . alive." Kathleen touched heels to Banshee's flanks and cantered past Juan Diego and his warriors, who stared at Mangas rolling with laughter on the ground. A hundred yards down the road, she glanced over her shoulder, but Mangas and his people were gone.

★ ★ ★ ★ ★

PART III
THE ROCKY MOUNTAINS

★ ★ ★ ★ ★

CHAPTER 18

On a late August afternoon, Kathleen scouted up the Green River with Banshee and her pack mule until she caught a glimpse of the Reed Trading Post on the north side of the Whiterocks River near its confluence with the Green and Uinta Rivers. Not much larger than a Navajo hogan, the one story log cabin was the first building she had seen in a month, but instead of approaching the goal that she had hunted for several weeks, she headed east into the cover of a rolling upland of piñon and juniper south of the Whiterocks River. After locating a likely ford, she retreated to a small glen dotted with sage and hobbled Banshee and the mule to let them crop their fill of grass while she waited inside the tree line for twilight. Then in the dim light after sunset, she gathered her animals, crossed to the north bank, and hid her camp in a copse of piñon trees.

With her animals short hobbled to keep them close to camp, she stripped off her wet pair of buckskins and hung them to dry over the branch of a tree. Wearing only shot bag and powder horn, she slipped through the dark to the river, carrying her rifle and one of her precious bars of lye soap. At the river, she scrubbed herself from head to toe, shaking in the icy cold water. Back at camp, she pulled on her spare pair of buckskins and fixed tortillas, beans, and a pot of coffee over a small fire. After dinner, she tied Banshee and the mule to adjoining piñons, banked the coals of her fire, and rolled out her bedding. Then she slipped under one of the thick buffalo robes she had purchased at Antoine Robidoux's trading post a month ago. Her wool blankets had proved no match for that first month of ever colder nights on the trail north from Taos Pueblo.

Fort Uncompahgre, that was what that scoundrel Robidoux had called his ramshackle collection of shacks surrounded by a thin palisade of sharpened logs on the Gunnison River. Men and their pretensions. When Kathleen had entered his store in her buckskin pants and shirt, he had looked her up and down before swearing in French and climbing out of his rocking chair. Without so much as a howdy-how-are-you, Robidoux had launched into a long harangue about his marriage to beautiful Carmel Benevedes, the adopted daughter of the governor of New Mexico. She pined, Robidoux had insisted, for his caresses in far off Santa Fe where present unhappy times with the damned Apaches had forced him to send her. Then he had boasted of his reputation among the women of St. Louis and claimed that an unending number of Indian women eagerly slid into his bed each night at the trading post.

Kathleen had needed warmer bedding and information about Colter's whereabouts, so she had pointed at two buffalo robes and asked their price in gold. While they haggled, Robidoux had dropped hints that there was a cheaper way to pay for the buffalo robes, but when she had taken a Mexican gold coin out of her shot bag and set it on the counter, he had bitten it and shoved the buffalo robes at her. At the sight of a smaller silver coin, he had allowed that Colter had passed through Fort Uncompahgre last summer on his way to beaver streams in the Uinta Mountains. Oh, that range lay somewhere up the Green River among the Utes. Prime beaver country. No, Colter had not come to Fort Uncompahgre this spring to trade his beaver pelts—plews Robidoux had called them—but Robidoux's good friends William Reed and Denis Julien had a trading post in the Uinta Basin just south of those mountains. Perhaps, Colter had traded there, or perhaps the Utes had killed him. Reed and Julien might know something, especially if she had more of those gold coins, and if she did not, well, Reed and Julien were lonely men far away from civilization. Kathleen had chucked the small silver coin into Robidoux's spittoon, and rewarded with a shower of Robidoux's curses, she had headed northwest.

So after a second month of slinking along ridges just below the crests, fording cold streams, and slipping through forests of fir and aspen with her eyes searching among trunks for movement, Kathleen camped once more in good cover. In the morning, she meant to go into Reed's Trading Post and find out what William Reed and Denis Julien knew about James Colter, but she did not look forward to this break in her isolation. Life in the timber and mountains was simple, dangerous, and clean. But this trading post, like Fort Robidoux and Rancho Taos before it, was sure to hold the taint of civilized men.

Kathleen rolled on her back and watched a twinkling star play peek-a-boo through rustling piñon boughs tossed about by a cold northeastern wind. Father Reynaldo had proved all too right about Rancho Taos, once a quiet Mexican ranching town dozing through most of the year between the vaqueros' spring and fall roundups, now bustling with Americans—trappers, fur traders, and schemers just like Robidoux. They had turned the town into a shabby assortment of trading posts, each part warehouse for beaver the fur traders bought from free trappers and for supplies to outfit those trappers for the next year, part saloon for these thirsty mountain men to drink away the cold of a trapping season minding trap lines set hip deep in winter streams, and part brothel to squeeze out of these drunken men whatever money they had left.

Thank goodness, it had been late June when Kathleen rode through Rancho Taos. Their money spent, the trappers had already headed their solitary ways into the mountains to scout fresh streams for signs of beaver, build log shacks for the winter, and trade with local Indian tribes for squaws to cook their meals and warm their beds. One of the Taos merchants had remembered a James Colter from the year before. A tall, lean, taciturn man, yes. Pox scars on his face. In a hurry, too. When none of the traders had any supplies left to grub stake him for the coming trapping season, still this Colter had ridden north. Perhaps, he had gone to the Gunnison River to pick up a stake from Antoine Robidoux. Perhaps, not. The merchant had never heard of Colter again, but if Kathleen had a taste for mountain men, well, the merchant had seen no call for her to traipse off into those God forsaken mountains just for one particular trapper. He had promised her good food and a warm bed at his trading post in Rancho Taos. Next spring, he had said, when the trappers came out of the mountains—big, fine, strapping woman that she was—she was a cinch to make plenty of money to pay him back for his hospitality. She had held her tongue and asked directions to the Gunnison River, but the greasy stench of the town had filled her nostrils for days thereafter.

Yes, Father Reynaldo had been correct about Rancho Taos. She missed his courtly speech and genteel manners—the sad faint smile that played about his lips. He had been a true friend, but she doubted that he missed her. Kathleen O'Dwyer, a woman, not Father Reynaldo, had single-handedly rescued Mangas Coloradas from fifty Mexican soldiers and saved Taos Pueblo from Apache vengeance. So the good father had helped gather the pack mule and supplies she needed to flee New Mexico, advised her about the dangers of the long journey, and wished her Godspeed. His concern for her was genuine. But what would he have done if she had somehow found a way to stay, going back to teaching the Tewa children and living out her days as a constant reminder of his many failures? One last fatherly embrace and a heartfelt goodbye, and they had parted friends. There was no going back to New Mexico.

So she had trekked northwest into the mountains and upland plains of the Utes. To go after a man she had once briefly known?

Kathleen sat up and, under the buffalo robe, hugged her knees. James Colter was tall. Small pox scars on his lean face. Blue eyes. Try as she might, Kathleen was hard put to remember much more about Colter's looks. Was that all there was to it? No, he had saved her life, not just once, but several times. But hadn't she saved his life, too? She had fought Comanche and killed their leader. She had helped kill German Joe Holtz and Billy Gap Tooth. Then she had nursed Colter through his injuries. Without her, he never would have made it to Taos: most likely died freezing somewhere in the mountains alone. Then he had left her. Their slate was even. She owed him nothing.

Yet now she followed him. Love? During the day, as she journeyed, she searched for cover in the forests and deserts to hide her movement. Was this valley the right pass? Or would it dead end against an insurmountable mountain face, forcing her to backtrack for days? There were not any maps to show the way. If she pitched camp near that spring, was the smell of her animals and food likely to draw grizzlies from the surrounding hills? The skills she had learned from Mangas about hiding her presence from others while tracking a quarry consumed her. Every decision was hers and hers alone. And she loved it, this wild, dangerous, free journey. She had a rifle, a horse, and a pack mule loaded with supplies. The mountain forests and upland grasslands stretched north forever for her to explore. Most nights, her belly was too full of fresh game she had shot and her muscles too full of aches and kinks to think beyond shelter for her animals and a warm bed roll for herself. Where was Colter during all of that? If she were in love, wouldn't she spend every waking moment dreaming of him?

Kathleen scratched a scalp itch and hoped she had not picked up head lice. There was no telling who had handled this buffalo robe before her. Maybe, she could find a lice comb at Reed's.

Maybe, wherever Colter was, maybe that was just a direction as good as any other. If that was true, then she could circle around Reed's Trading Post and head into the Uintas. If she found Colter sometime this fall, all well and good. If not, she could ride into Reed's next spring when mountain men from the Green River and its tributaries gathered for rendezvous. One of them was bound to have word of Colter. In any event, fall would shortly paint the hardwood leaves a riot of colors, and winter would strip them bare soon afterwards. She needed a sheltered mountain glen while there was still time to build a log cabin to keep herself and her animals warm and dry through the winter. Somewhere with good water and enough game to augment her stores of beans, jerky, and corn meal. Somewhere away from the eyes of unwanted men—white and red. Maybe after a peaceful winter alone, she would know whether to go on searching for James Colter, or be done with him, strike out in a new direction.

But was she done with Colter? That was a hard question, but not because she still longed for him. No, if anything, his memory scarcely stirred her. But the memory of her love for him stirred her. What a shock that love had been! Emotion running riot with her senses. Color and sound. Scent and touch. All of life charged with an embarrassing elation.

Why had that love so embarrassed her?

Even when its grip on her senses had made her tremble and gasp, she had felt this deep, shame-faced embarrassment. She had often heard that love had the power to make a young girl take leave of her senses. But she knew now that was not true. If anything, it had made her senses too much with her. Yes, like a young girl in her first surging blush of youth. That was what had embarrassed her, for she was a grown woman when love struck her. While love had filled her with that dizzying ecstasy, her mature and sober good sense had known that this passion was out of place and out of time with her adult womanhood, as surely as if she had fallen back into playing with dolls and singing nursery rhymes. Perhaps, at Taos Pueblo, when Colter had first packed his gear for the mountains, that was why Kathleen had kept her silence.

So what did she want from love this time? Whatever it was—if anything at all—not the mad surging love of a girl. A girl in love lived only for love. Afraid of the strength and wisdom required of a woman, a girl in love retreated, like a child, into an emotion; for such love demanded anything that fed it. All restraint, all principles, all the hard learned values that defined an individual's soul were cast aside. That was an abdication of self that a girl outgrew if she was ever to become a woman. No, if love was to stir Kathleen again, this time it must stir her with a passion appropriate for a woman. It must fill her mind as well as heart. It must not demand that she take leave of her good judgment. It must flow in harmony with her good judgment—or it would not stir her at all. Would she . . . could she . . . feel that sort of love for Colter?

Kathleen lay down, making sure the buffalo robe covered her rifle and powder horn, as well as herself. Colter or no Colter, here in the West, what she must have were a well-oiled rifle and dry powder. In dreams that night, the buffalo woman was a naked, copper giant towering above dark mountains that surrounded Kathleen. Her black hair a billowing cloud blotting out the sun, the buffalo woman chanted a summons, part blessing and part curse. Again, a harsh cold wind was in Kathleen's face, whipping her eyes with snow. She rode Banshee into the teeth of this blinding white storm, trying to follow the wailing cries of a woman giving birth in agony, but the cries seemed to come from all around her. Cold, terrified, she chased first one way and then another. The driving snow turned crimson, and swollen with pain, the woman's cries echoed from all directions off the mountains. Banshee stumbled on icy crimson snow, so Kathleen dismounted and led him. Her nostrils filled with the stench of blood and placenta and a vast rising female fecundity. Despite her terror, she followed that stench like a wolf bitch tracing her own scent back to the den. The cries grew louder and louder, and the reek of birthing female ever more powerful. Fear a kicking, nauseating mass in her stomach, she kept going, panting and gasping, drawn by the chanting buffalo woman to follow those agonized cries. Awakening, Kathleen knew she had no time to rest. She must go deeper into grey-blue mountains, and she must go now.

With the bright morning sun behind her, Kathleen reined Banshee to a halt and looked down at the Reed Trading Post a hundred yards away beside the juncture of the Uintas, Green, and Whiterocks Rivers. Birch and cottonwood grew too dense in the bottom land along the rivers, so approaching the trading post, she had stayed in the arid hills dotted with juniper and piñon north of the Whiterocks River. Still, finding the trading post had proven no trouble: she had trusted her nose to follow the odor of smoke pouring out of the cabin chimney. Mangas had once said that no Indian, whether free roaming Apache or town dwelling Tewa, ever built a fire as wasteful and revealing as a white man. High water lines darkened tree boles beside the log cabin. Reed and Julien had built too close to the rivers. Two pairs of horses were tied out front of the cabin. Each pair consisted of a saddled horse and a loaded pack animal. Were Reed and Julien about to set out on an expedition, or did the fur traders have company? Kathleen adjusted the set of the large hunting knife belted to her waist and the smaller one inside her right moccasin. Then she touched heels to Banshee's flanks and rode down to the trading post.

The smell of frying bacon filled the cold river air, so Reed and Julien or someone was up and stirring. Broken glass, colored beads, and shards of shattered clay littered the ground all around the cabin. While she looped the reins of her own animals to the hitching rail, she watched the cabin door. She heard a deep, rich, bass voice say, "Hey, Bill, you got company," quickly followed by the clatter of a skillet on stone. Topped by a coonskin hat, a white man's large, round face with thick, sagging jowls and a huge nose thrust out of one of the two cabin windows. The man looked Kathleen over, let out a shrill whistle, and pulled his head inside the cabin. "It's a woman." His voice was hoarse with a nasally twang and not nearly as deep as the first man's. "A Goddamn, big as creation, living, breathing white woman. But she's all fitted out like a man." A thin man of medium height and sandy hair appeared in the doorway. He wore a homespun grey cotton shirt, butternut trousers held up with black suspenders, and heavy boots. Behind him, peering over his shoulder, was the grinning face of the big-nosed mountain man. "Morning, ma'am," the sandy-haired man said. "Name's William Reed. Bill will do. You're welcome to share our breakfast, if you've a mind to."

"Morning," Kathleen said. "I've already eaten, but a cup of coffee would suit just fine."

"Come on in." Bill Reed stepped aside to let her pass. "Over yonder on the hearth, pot's good and hot. Cup's on the wall. Help yourself." Though his eyes took in her buckskins and rifle, he had not forgotten his manners. So Kathleen stepped into the cabin. To get to the fireside, she had to pass by the grinning mountain man, who rolled his eyes as if her nearness made him faint. At the hearth, she set her Hawken against a table and keeping an eye on all around her, took a tin cup off a peg in the wall and poured coffee in it. Most of the cabin was taken up with rough, heavily stained, wooden counters and shelves. Several had iron traps of various sizes, others wooden crates filled with beads and other trade goods, but most of the tables and shelves were full of empty liquor bottles and clay jugs. Animal pelts were tacked here and there to the walls. Over against the far wall where he had a good view out one of the front windows, another mountain man sat on a three-legged stool, smoking a long-barreled clay pipe. He was an old black man whose scant hair looked like swatches of white wire knitted to his temples. His face, the dark, burnt color of a fire-hardened Indian spear, was heavily weathered. Almost lost in the face's deeply etched lines and creases, a scar twisted through his left eyebrow and onto his cheek. His right ear was no more than a gnawn-off stump. But his shoulders were broad and unbowed. His stomach showed no trace of a pot, and even sitting down, he looked to be at least as tall as Kathleen. Leaning against the wall beside him was an old trade flintlock. When he bobbed his head, she nodded back. "Hey, hey, Israel, I spotted her first," the grinning white mountain man said. He was a couple of inches shorter than Kathleen but built like a badger—thick shoulders and arms with powerful haunches and calves. His dark-brown matted beard was shiny with grease, and when he stepped closer to Kathleen, he reeked of bacon, chewing tobacco, and a whiff of liquor. "I done staked my claim to her plew."

"Don't pay no attention to Big-Nose Allen, ma'am," Bill Reed said. "He talks mighty big, but he ain't generally no harm to nobody this early in the morning. How can I help you this morning—Miss?"

"Yeah, Big-Nose Joe Allen, that's what they call me," the white mountain man said and tweaked his own nose. "You know what they say about a man with a big nose, don't you?" Sipping her coffee, Kathleen looked Allen in the face. So, the filthy business had begun again. Wherever there were men, there was a Big-Nosed Joe Allen, swarming like a coyote to a hunk of choice meat someone had hung too low in a tree—face tense with that half-friendly, half-intimidating grin. It did not matter whether she wore buckskin trousers or a proper cotton dress with a high starched collar. She was alone. Over by the door, little William Reed's brows knit in anger, but his eyes showed more than a little fear. By the far wall, the other mountain man sat and smoked his pipe, watching Kathleen and Big-Nose Allen and William Reed by the door. This was the situation she had feared last night, but now that it was at hand, she felt a reckless thrill that did not surprise her. The pounding of her heart, the gun metal taste in her mouth were by now a familiar excitement, akin to sighting down the barrel of her rifle at a fine buck. She knew why some men spent their lives in the army courting death for that sense of power. "I do not give a damn what they say."

Joe Allen's face turned scarlet red. While the black man Israel shook with laughter and slapped his thigh, she turned to Bill Reed. "My name is Kathleen O'Dwyer. I am wondering if you have ever heard of a trapper called James Colter?"

"Yes ma'am, he came through here last spring to trade his plews." Reed looked at Israel, who smoked his pipe and, smiling, blew smoke rings at Big-Nose Allen. "He's trapping up in the Uintas, ain't he, Israel?"

"Kate, so that's what they call you?" Allen, hands on his hips, sidled next to Kathleen close enough for his foul breath to make her grimace. "Well, Kate, you may not hear tell of me before, but I can make you forget all about that Colter feller. I'm the meanest, fightingest, ring-tailed roarer this side of the Mississippi and a whale of a lover to boot. I'm French, you know. A hundred percent Cajun. Built for hard fighting, good loving, and sweet whiskey."

"Speaking of whiskey," Israel said, knocked his pipe against the wall, and set it on a countertop. "Big-Nose, you been drinking this early in the morning?"

"Well, I ain't saying I have, and I ain't saying I ain't." Allen glanced at Israel and Bill Reed. Then he winked at Kathleen and, slipping his left arm around her shoulders, pulled her close. "But that ain't a bad idea. What say you and me slip off in the woods and share a drop or two of old Bill's liver ailment?"

"Whoa there!" Bill Reed pointed a finger at Allen. "You ain't going to roughhouse a woman in my place."

"I ain't aiming to roughhouse her none." Allen stared at the smaller Bill Reed and grinned. "I'm just aiming to show her a little friendly welcome. Nobody best get in my way."

"Why, Big-Nose!" Israel stood up and took a step toward Allen and Kathleen. "You have been drinking and ain't shared none with me. Here, you sweet-talking me most this last week, ever since I gave that old fever that had hold of me the slip." He took another step. "Trying to talk me into going partners with you this season. And now you done hide a bottle from me. Ain't right, no way." Israel advanced another step. "I expect you and me ought to go outside and settle this, just you and me—if we's going be partners."

"Keep back, Israel." Allen's grip tightened on Kathleen's left shoulder. His other hand settled on the hilt of the knife at his hip. "Me and Kate's going outside by ourselves. You keep away if you know what's good for you."

"Kate, I ain't going to let him hurt you," Israel said, but he stopped his advance. "Don't you be scared."

"Now why would I be scared?" Kathleen smiled at Allen, who grinned. Then she stamped on the arch of his left foot, knocked his hand off her shoulder, and spun in a tight circle, slamming her right elbow into his eye. Grunting in pain, he stumbled away with one hand to his eye. Crowding forward, she knocked him off balance again with her shoulder and jerked the knife out of her own belt. When he planted his feet, she slashed upwards and chopped off his nose and a good deal of flesh off the hand he held to his eye. Howling, he put both hands to his face, but blood gushed through his fingers down his beard. Then Kathleen booted him between the legs and stepped back, letting Allen fall forward on his ruined face. Dropping on his back, she yanked his head up by the hair and slipped the knife blade against his throat.

"You still want to go for a walk in the woods with me?"

He gasped and choked. She pressed the knife against his throat, drawing a thin line of crimson.

"Nah," Allen said. Kathleen released her hold and stood up, wiping blood off her knife on the shoulder of Joe Allen's leather shirt.

"Hoo-whee! Guess we'll call you Chop-Nose Joe Allen from here on." Israel laughed and prodded Allen with his toe. "Get on out of here. Go on. I never was your partner, and I ain't never going be your partner. So git!"

Clutching his bleeding face and gagging, Allen climbed to his feet and staggered toward the door. Israel followed hard on Allen's heels, shoving him whenever he paused to spit blood. Bill Reed came along behind Israel, carrying an old Pennsylvania long rifle with an ugly sawn down barrel. Kathleen grabbed her rifle from beside the fireplace and headed outside with them.

Israel stood under the eve of the cabin roof, chuckling and mocking Allen's efforts to clear blood out of his throat. Allen staggered to the horses and untied a pair of scruffy mustangs, not much bigger than ponies. Leaning against the saddled one, he mopped his face with the sleeve of his shirt and looked back at Israel, Bill Reed, and Kathleen. His eyes narrowed, and he spat pink phlegm.

"This ain't over, you whoring bitch."

Kathleen leveled her rifle at his face, which turned pale white. "Then I will end it right here."

Blood oozing down his beard, Allen stare wide-eyed at the muzzle of the fifty-four-caliber Hawken while Israel slapped his side and cackled with laughter.

"Hoo-whee, Chop-Nose! Best hush your dirty mouth. Kate here going to change your name to Hole-in-the-Head Joe Allen. Yeah, boy. What's the matter, Chop-Nose? Where's that old ring-tailed roarer Cajun now?"

"Miss O'Dwyer, ma'am?" With just one hand on the barrel, Bill Reed held up the rifle he had brought out of the cabin. "This here's Joe's rifle. I know he deserves killing, but please don't. I'm sure he takes back all them foul words, don't you, Joe? Joe, speak up before she blows your dang head off." Joe Allen gulped and nodded his head, but his eyes never left the muzzle of Kathleen's rifle. "It's over now, ain't it, Joe?" Allen nodded.

"Say it." With her thumb, Kathleen cocked her rifle hammer.

"It's over," Allen said, but the rifle barrel stayed locked on his face. Sweat stood out on his forehead. The air filled with the stink of his fear. "It's over, ma'am. I take it all back, every word. Please."

Kathleen lowered the rifle. Joe Allen turned and flinging one arm over the pommel of his saddle, doubled over and retched out whatever he had eaten that morning, which sent Israel into another fit of laughter. Bill Reed pointed Allen's rifle in the air and fired. Then he tossed the weapon at Allen's feet. "Get on out of here, Joe."

Allen picked up his rifle and with a groan, pulled himself astride his horse. He sat for a moment, eyeing Kathleen. Then he kicked his horse's flanks and leading his pack horse, galloped away.

"Well, that's over and done with." Bill Reed looked at Kathleen and extended his right hand. "He's a no-account skunk for certain, but he's one of my customers. His kind bring in the beaver. I couldn't do without them. But truth be told, nary a one of them's fit for decent folks—no offense, Israel."

"None taken." Israel smiled at Kathleen. "Never claimed to be anything special. Just a free man."

"Well, I thank you for your help." Kathleen returned the old man's smile. He carried himself with a rakish bravado, but he stood his ground.

"And I thank you for not shooting one of my customers," Bill Reed said and swept his hand toward the cabin. "I'd be obliged if you'd finish your cup of coffee. I'll be happy to tell you all I know about that there James Colter."

The excitement that had wound tight her muscles drained out of Kathleen, and the familiar weakness that came after danger crept into her knees and arms. A hollow knot in her stomach faded away, leaving her a tad queasy, and juices gurgled through her bowels once more.

"Thank you. I believe I will."

CHAPTER 19

As it turned out, Bill Reed did not claim to know much more. Colter had come into Reed's to trade his beaver last spring. He had swapped most of his beaver for supplies and trade goods for the upcoming season. Unlike most other mountain men who drank away their extra cash, Colter had taken a promissory note for the rest of his plews, but he had entrusted the note to Reed's partner, Denis Julien, who each summer took that year's beaver east to St. Louis. Julien had promised to deposit Colter's money in a St. Louis bank. Then Colter had headed up the Whiterocks River. That was all Reed said he knew, so Kathleen pulled up another stool beside Israel and asked him about Colter. The old mountain man sat smoking for a long time before he answered.

"Yeah, I knows him. Trapped alongside him on the upper Green last season. We wasn't exactly partners—Colter don't seem to partner close with any man. I ran my trap line, he ran his, but we look out for each other just the same. He ain't too big a fool. Not like most white men. Ain't too proud to sit and smoke with old black Israel—ask me for help if he need it. Then again, most men what come up these mountains ain't like flat-landers."

"Do you know where he is now?" Kathleen asked.

Israel shifted on his stool. "He ain't like that bastard Chop-Nose either. I like saying that name—Chop-Nose. Got a right smart ring to it. But ain't near as pretty as my name—Israel

184

Baptiste Mongrief. Used to be Certaine, but I changed it long ago. Back afore I come west. Way back in Louisiana. That's where I'm from. I'm Creole. Old Chop-Nose always claim he's Cajun, but he never speak a word of French, not one. I never believe him. Allen ain't no Cajun name. He just old Mississippi gutter trash talking big. He—"

"Do you know anything else about James Colter?" Kathleen sat forward and put a hand on Israel's knee. "I must know."

Puffing hard on his pipe, Israel stared at her hand. Then he met Kathleen's eyes and smiled, but his eyes were sad, betraying the smile he forced. "Kate, I'm a married man. Got me a wife somewheres." His eyes grew dark and brooding. "I can't be holding hands with no other woman. I can't."

"Israel, please?" Kathleen said, uncertain whether she was asking about Colter or beseeching Israel's pardon. Israel took a long pull on his pipe and then sent plumes of smoke shooting out his nose.

"You ain't going to let this go, is you? Nah, not you. Once you sets your aim on something, you don't back off. I sees that about you already, Kate O'Dwyer." Then a twinkle came back in his eyes. "But you best take your hand off my knee so I can tell the story right. Too distracting, even for an old timer like me."

Blushing, Kathleen sat back. Israel dug around in his shirt and pulled out a small leather pouch. Loosening the bag's drawstring, he dipped the pipe in the pouch. Tamping down loose tobacco, he sucked on the pipe stem until the fresh tobacco caught fire.

"I trap with him last winter on the upper Green, in mountain creeks south of Antelope Flat. We took in a heap of beaver plews, but nowheres near what they used to be up the Green. Still, we made do. Colter makes a good partner. He sets his traps right and don't whine about standing half the day in freezing water up to his ass. Good feller in a pinch, too. Shoots straight but just as soon sidestep a tussle if he sees it a coming. Don't talk much, though. I kind of like that. Can't stand a partner who spends all day jawing. Feller ought to say what he means in as few words as possible and leave it at that." Israel took a long pull on his pipe.

Over by the fireplace, Bill Reed jabbed an iron poker at smoldering logs, sending sparks flying. "Like you, huh, Israel?"

Israel grinned and slapped his thigh. "That's right. Colter don't say much, but he means what he say. He got along with the Utes and Ourays. Never tried to short them in a trade, the way most white men do—no offense, Bill."

"Tit for tat, we're even now, Israel." Reed nodded at Kathleen. "You going to tell her the whole story? You done started in."

"I sees how you chawed a ring around the tree without getting to the heartwood." Israel met Reed's glare, and Kathleen eyed both men.

"You best finish it," Reed said. "All of it."

"I expect you're right." Israel fiddled with his pipe.

Kathleen sat up straight. "What?"

"Colter got along with the Utes and Ourays, like I say." Israel knocked the clay pipe against a stool leg, dumping ashes on the floor. "Last fall, a band of Utes show up at our camp wanting to trade. Seems they'd just finished a big palaver up north with the Shoshone. This one buck had a Lakota woman the Shoshones had traded him. Little bitty thing, hardly more than a child. Fourteen, fifteen at most. Pretty though. Shoshones got her from the Crows, who stole her a few years ago from her own people. This here Ute buck had figured on her being a camp slave for his squaw, but he wasn't too happy with her—too small, I reckon. She couldn't speak a word of Ute, English neither. Colter took a shine to her. Traded a block of tobacco for her." Israel sighed and looked out the window.

"Go on." Kathleen was surprised how flat her voice sounded—not a trace of anger or hurt. She told herself that she had half expected something like this. Colter was a free man. She told herself she had no right to anger, no right to tears. She told herself she would be damned before she would show either anger or tears in front of these men.

"He hung onto her through the winter," Israel said. "Long about spring, her belly begun to show. He could have traded her back to the Utes or another trapper, but he kept her. Took her with him up the Whiterocks."

To replenish her stores, Kathleen set a five-pound sack of coffee and, since Reed was out of sugar as well as combs, a clay jar of honey on the main counter. For winter in the mountains, she also picked out a heavy wool capote, fur-lined leather mittens, and snow shoes. His eyes full of pity, Reed took what she offered without haggling. Kathleen stifled the urge to backhand him. Then she slung the new gear over her shoulder and headed out the door.

Outside, Israel sat astride a chestnut mare with the tether of his grey pack animal tied to his saddle. Kathleen set about stowing the gear on her mule—all too conscious of Israel's watchful, heavy-lidded gaze, while she unlaced leather bindings, peeled back a corner of the canvas shell, shoved new supplies into place, and tied the whole load tight. She took her time to make sure everything fit snugly. Loose cargo would bang and clatter, drawing unwanted attention and slipping back and forth, wearing out the mule. Then she unhitched her animals, mounted Banshee, and pointed him northwest up the Whiterocks toward the soaring grey-blue peaks of the distant Uintas.

Israel, her ears told her, fell in line about thirty yards behind her.

They traveled that way for the rest of the morning, but by noon Kathleen was tired of exposing her back to a man with a rifle while she tried to keep a sharp eye in front of her for the likes of Joe Allen or a Ute lying in ambush. Israel had meant to help her at Reed's, but he was a free trapper, a man by his own admission not like the "decent folks" of the flat lands. From the little she had seen of him, she knew he was moody, like most other mountain men, given to fitful swings of humor and temper, inured to violence, and accustomed to acting on the merest whim. She reined Banshee to a halt and dismounted. With her rifle ready in the crook of her left arm, she loosed the cinch strap around Banshee's girth while Israel approached.

"You reckon it's time for noon coffee?" Israel swung down off his mare and balancing his rifle across his saddle, loosened the strap on his own horse.

"And if I do," Kathleen said, "what makes you think you are invited?"

"Course I'm invited." Israel leaned his rifle against a stump and then turned to hobbling his mare. "I'm your partner." Then he loosened the cinch straps on his grey and knelt to hobble it. Kathleen stared at him. Why of all the brazen effrontery she had ever seen men attempt, this surely took top rung on the ladder. He looked over his shoulder at her. "You going to make the fire or stand there gawking?"

"Partner?" Kathleen jabbed her index finger at him. "I am not your partner."

"You going to find Colter, ain't you? You aiming to partner up with him. Well, him and me are partners. So that makes you and me partners, too."

"I never said anything about going partners with Colter." She felt her voice tighten.

"Never said you did." Israel straightened up with a groan. "Old knees full of rheumitiz. Still, you leave out of Reed's hunting Colter. I ain't sure you mean to hook up partners with him or shoot him, but I'm his partner. So I best go along with you."

Kathleen put her right hand on the action of her rifle. "Partners? Do not read too much into that."

Israel laughed and winked at her. "Kate, nears as I can figure it, I'm sixty-three, maybe sixty-four years old. That fire's banked pretty low in me. Unless you go stirring it up yourself, you ain't got nothing to worry about."

Shaking her head, Kathleen rolled her tongue around her teeth. Israel had an honest look in his eyes, like the old Mexican peasant who had brought supplies to her schoolhouse in Santa Fe. Israel was louder, but he carried himself with the same dignity. She took two steps forward and extended her right hand. "All right, partners."

Israel shook her hand. "Something tells me you still might shoot James Colter."

"I might at that."

For the rest of the day, Kathleen and Israel followed the White-rocks as it rose northwest. On the morning of the second day, the air was crisp and cold, turning their breath to smoky vapor. Groves of aspen and birch, leaves already tinged with yellow streaks, claimed more and more of the land from stumpy piñon and juniper. Flats-loving antelope gave way to mule deer marking areas for the fall rut. Blue piñon jays had to fight with highland red squirrels for nuts.

On horseback or afoot in camp, Kathleen and Israel kept a sharp eye all around, for grizzlies stalked creek beds and trees in growing numbers, grazing like cows in the high yellow grass or foraging for fish and nuts and the dregs of summer's chokeber-ries, ready to charge like roaring silver-brown landslides at all who approached. Most dangerous of all were pregnant females or sows with this year's cubs. On the trail, Kathleen and Israel gave bears a wide berth, and at night, they hung their parfleches of corn meal, sugar, and jerky high in the trees and slept with the hammers of their rifles cocked. Once, they awoke to the screaming of their horses just in time to fire at a massive dark bulk that reared beside Israel's grey pack horse. It fell over bawling and roaring in a thrashing ball that smashed brush and snapped the trunks of small trees before it lay gurgling out the last of its savage blood. In the morning, they skinned it. Kathleen dug out the bear's claws for a necklace.

"A three-year-old male," Israel said, "fresh out on his own, not as tasty as a black bear, but still good eating." So they butchered what they could load on the pack animals and fried up bear steaks for breakfast.

"A tad gamey meat," Kathleen said and picked her teeth with a twig.

That day, rapids marked the sharp rise of the river. No more than twelve yards wide, the river spilled from clear blue pool to pool among lichen-splotched granite rocks washed white by frothing water. Kathleen remarked that these rocks must have given the river its name.

"Somebody named it Whiterocks," Israel said. "Be they Ute or Ouray or white man. Don't know the Injun name for the river, but most of the lands west of the Big Muddy still Injun lands. Still got their Injun names. White man ain't sunk his fingers deep in it yet. Changed it around to suit him and only him. This land's still clean and free."

"Do you hate all white people, Israel?"

"Nah. Ain't got nothing against white women." Israel flashed a smile. "Seems their feet caught in the same trap as blacks and Injuns. White man claim to own them all, but ain't nobody got a claim to him." Israel batted at some gnats around his face. "I don't hate all white men, neither. Here and there, I run into a few good ones. Colter's one. But on the whole, I got no use for them."

Kathleen looked around, trying to fix in her mind images of this vast wild country. She was privileged and humbled to see its pristine splendor. "Someday," she said, "they will swarm across these mountains and plains and rivers clear to the Pacific Ocean. Their God-given birthright, that's all the talk back East."

"Yeah," Israel said. "But I'll be dead by then."

So they climbed to the feet of the mountains. Here, birch and aspen were cloud banks of saffron and yellow among green cedar, darker fir, and blue-green spruce. Early frosts had burnt brown the withered grass.

"Winter's coming on early," Israel said. "Going be a bad one."

"I have not seen any sign of beaver yet," Kathleen said. "Are you sure Colter is up here?"

"Lower river's been trapped out since twenty-five." Israel pointed at distant peaks. "Colter's gone high, searching for plews, up where no free trapper's been. Utes been up there. Some say there's a pretty little lake at the head waters, but Utes don't like to winter up high. Ain't likely they trapped it."

"Are you certain he has gone up there?"

Israel shrugged. "Where else you going to hunt him this late in the year? It's either go ahead or go back. But Colter ain't at Reed's."

So for the next three days, they climbed higher into grey-blue mountains. The stands of aspen and birch thinned, giving way to blankets of fir and lodgepole pine on sharply angled slopes. Not far above her head, Kathleen saw trees play out entirely. Every once in a while, she saw moving specks of white way up among dark-grey granite faces below the snow-capped heights.

"Some kind of goats, least that's what some white men crazy enough to climb up there say," Israel said, "but what them crit-

191

ters find to eat up there only God knows. Utes say they're ghosts. Could be they're right."

The river angled northwest up a cut between peaks and then flattened in a high, wide, densely forested valley. Off their right, a little creek pooled behind a neatly kept beaver dam. Ten to fifteen miles ahead, mountains climbed once more. As the sun faded in the west, a fierce cold wind blew off these far mountains. Still, they had seen no sign of James Colter. So Kathleen gathered wood and kindling while Israel unloaded their animals and hobbled them for the night. Then Israel opened his strike-a-light bag and fished around for flint and steel. Kathleen dumped an armful of dead wood beside Israel, who scraped the steel bar with his piece of flint, knocking sparks into a mound of dry grass and pine needles.

"Israel, do you think it is a waste for me to come up here searching for this man?" A flame caught and then sank to orange embers in a smoky cloud, but Israel blew on the embers until fire burned strongly. Then he broke wood into short sticks and chunks of bark to feed the fire.

"A waste?" Israel laid one stick on the burning mound, then another. "Nah, searching for someone you love ain't never a waste." He smiled and pointed a stick at her. "I know what you're fixing to say—that you ain't never say you love James Colter, that you're just hunting him, that maybe you're going to shoot him when you find him. Sure sounds like love to me."

"Have you ever been in love, Israel?" But when Israel licked his lips and looked away, Kathleen hastened to say, "Of course, you have. You said you were a married man the first time I met you. I'm sorry."

Israel fed more sticks in the fire and fanned the flames with his hat. When the wood crackled, he sat back and stared at the flames.

"Yeah, I'm married—was married. I don't know where she is

or if she's even alive. But I love her, alive or dead. I'll go on loving her forever I guess. White folks say, 'till death do ye part,' but that seems too short to me." He dug around in his coat pocket and pulled out his pipe. Kathleen watched the dark mood grow on Israel while he loaded tobacco and lit it with a twig from the fire. "We lived on a Creole plantation down the delta country around New Orleans. Old Marse Certaine, he was the owner. Grow rice, indigo, some sweet cane. Celeste and me grow up working the fields. Everyone knows we belong together, even old Marse. She was the prettiest thing ever was. And me, I grow up big and strong—head like a rock. But I knew enough to know I love her." He settled cross legged facing the flames and puffed on his pipe.

"Old Marse Certaine's a betting man. Most Creoles is, but Marse Certaine got the bug bad. If a mule drop a turd, old Marse bet on the color fly going to light on it first. Throw half his crop away betting each year, old Marse Certaine do."

"Your last name was Certaine once, was it not?" Kathleen tried to make her voice light and cheerful to draw the twinkle back into Israel's eyes. "I have heard that French Creoles often intermarry with their slaves. Were you his kin?"

"Nah, he ain't no kin to me." He hugged his elbows as if to draw anger like a coat against bitter cold wind. "Plantation Creoles take their sport now and then with black women. Truth be told, half the field hands and house servants sprung from the same tree as the master. Cajuns hold that against delta Creoles, saying ain't none of them really white no more. But plantation Creoles look down their long French noses at them up-river Cajuns. Creoles say Cajuns ain't nothing but trash the English swept out of Canada and dumped in the back waters of Louisiana. Anyways, plantation Creoles make sure the bloodlines living in the big house stay good and white. You got a drop of black blood—then you can't own no land in Louisiana. You can't own nothing." Israel took a long pull on his pipe. Kathleen looked around for the coffee pot. Maybe, if she got something warm in him, the mood would let him go.

"Marse Certaine like me 'cause I'm big and strong. Takes to fighting me with slaves from other plantations round home. Say if I won, he give me Celeste. So I win every fight, beat the living tar out of every one. Marse Certaine make a heap of money betting on me. So he say the words over Celeste and me. Give us a cabin of our own. We have two childs. Jean and Marie. Some years go by. Then I lose a fight. Other feller chaw my ear off and whip me good—broke two of my ribs. Marse Certaine lose a heap of money. So he sells Celeste and my younguns.

"When I heal up, I take off. Just go looking for Celeste. Got no idea where she is. Sneak into plantations all over Louisiana. Ain't hard to sneak in, but hell getting out. Get caught, sent home, get beat. Don't give a damn. Take off again. This go on a year or more. Marse Certaine say he going to fix me so I ain't got no use for a woman, maybe then I stay put. So this time, I kill him and take off. Get across the Mississippi and keep going clean to Arkansas, up in the Ozarks. Never see mountains before. So I stays there a while. Take up with some Osages. They good people. They learn me how to shoot and hunt. Want to give me a woman, but I say, 'No thank you, I'm looking for Celeste.' Then whites burn the Osage's villages. Run them and me off. I take out west again." Israel looked at Kathleen. His eyes were hard, full of self-loathing. "But I give up looking for Celeste. I tell myself I'm a free man. I tell myself to start a new life out here. That's nigh thirty year ago. I didn't know it then, but that's when the waste begin for me—when I give up looking for Celeste."

Kathleen looked away, but she felt his eyes on her, demanding that she look at him.

"You never found love again?"

"I found what passes for it, a time or two. A Mojave squaw when trapping's good down the Colorado. A Flathead up on the Snake for four whole seasons. Then when the beaver play out, I'd move on. Leaving them behind's easy after letting go of Celeste. By then, I'm old and see the waste I done make of my life. Now, you thinking about making the same waste of yours."

"I did not leave him." She wondered why she had no tears— not for herself and not for Israel. Had she changed that much since she left St. Louis? She looked at the hands on her knees: rough, calloused, dirt under cracked nails. They were powerful hands. She felt hard strength in her arms and shoulders. She could hold a fifty-four Hawken against her cheek and aim it still as a rock. Break a man's jaw with one blow. But had she driven out all that was tender and fine in herself?

She felt the dark mood that held Israel prisoner seep into her bones. She felt neither cold nor warmth, just a vast aching nothingness. Maybe, this was all that Colter had felt when he had seen the need in her eyes. This nothingness would have made it easy for him to leave her. And maybe, filled with this aching nothingness, she had come up here just to look him in the eye and walk away first this time.

Israel stood and wandered into the dark night. By the ember glowing at the end of his pipe, Kathleen marked where he sat down beside the Whiterocks. Instead of fixing coffee, she banked the fire and laid out their bed rolls a few feet apart near their horses. Then she pulled the buffalo robe across herself and her rifle. In a moment, she was asleep.

CHAPTER 20

The morning dawned cold and windy with a sky solid grey from horizon to horizon. The black mood was still on Israel, and when Kathleen asked, over chunks of bear meat and corn bread, whether these clouds meant an early snow, he shrugged. After breaking camp, they traveled a short way into the valley, until Kathleen reined in Banshee and pointed up a stream to her left. Beside her, Israel stared a moment and then nodded. Two hundred yards away, a naked white man stood hip deep in a beaver pool with his back to them: James Colter.

Even at two hundred yards, Kathleen knew his shock of brown hair, the lean wiry set of his shoulders and back, but she felt no surge of overwhelming emotion, no catch in her breath. She felt a twinge of pride at getting this close without his sensing her, but that was all. She had come a long way in a year and half from the school teacher who had set out from St. Louis in a sturdy new pair of boots. She swung off her horse and tied it and the pack mule to a tree. In a moment, Israel did the same. Then rifles in hand, using the cover of willow and birch trees crowding the stream banks, they glided quietly around to one side of Colter.

Thirty yards away, Kathleen squatted on her heels and watched Colter through a gap in the trees. Sitting cross legged beside her, Israel dug out his pipe. A few feet up the far bank of the pond, Colter's buckskins and moccasins were hung across a bush. His rifle lay propped beside them. Kathleen watched

Colter, pale and blowing in freezing water, set a beaver trap.

Hung around his neck on separate leather thongs were a heavy wooden mallet and a stoppered horn. With his left arm, he clutched four thick sticks, each about a foot and a half long, and one long, five-foot stake. In his right hand, he held a double-sprung steel trap by its six-foot chain. Between his teeth was a slender, willowy, three-foot-long branch with the bark stripped away to reveal bright, yellow-white, fresh wood. Stepping carefully, he waded close to shore until water was only halfway up his shins.

Then he took a pair of the short sticks from under his left arm. These sticks were tied together at one end by a leather string, while another string dangled from one stick at the other end. Colter slipped one spring of the trap between the tied ends of the sticks and grabbed the free ends of the sticks to squeeze the vise. With the trap spring fully depressed, he looped the free string around the sticks in his hands and tied the vise shut. Then he squeezed the trap's other spring with the other stick vise, but held it shut with his left hand. Carefully, he set the round trigger plate under its dog and released enough tension with his left hand vise to prime the trap. Then he lowered the trap into the water in front of his feet and released both vises. Straightening up, but without moving his feet, he took the bait branch from his teeth and stuck it in the bank so the slender stick bent over the trap hidden by the water. Then Colter unstoppered the horn around his neck and poured beaver stink on bait stick, bank, and water around the trap. Then he recapped the horn. Backing into the pond to the length of the trap chain, he stood chest deep in water and used the mallet to drive the long stake into the mud through the chain ring.

With his wooden vises stowed under his left arm again, he circled away from the trap and waded ashore next to his clothes. Shivering, Colter shook like a dog to wring water off his blue-white flesh. Then he reached for his shirt.

"You are getting mighty careless up this high," Kathleen called out, snapping Colter's head around. With a curse, he flung away his wooden vises and snatched up his rifle. "Or did the water freeze your brain?"

"You better hope that's all it froze," Israel said and laughed. "Or you mighta wasted a trip up here."

Turning away, Colter leaned his rifle against the bush and busied himself with putting on his clothes. More weathered by sun and wind, the skin of his face and hands was a shade darker, and a couple of new scars showed pink across his white arms and legs. If anything, he was skinnier than Kathleen remembered—all bony joints strung together by wire muscles. His mud-caked feet seemed ridiculously small for such a tall man.

When he looked at them, his jaw was set tighter, and the crow's-feet around his eyes were etched a little deeper than she remembered, but his eyes were still cold blue. In them, wariness was still there, but some of its edge was gone, like a knife worn by rough use. A haunted inward-turning stare dulled his eyes' clarity.

Once, she knew, seeing those eyes corroded by that haunted stare would have touched her with pain, but here, she felt no surge of love, no need to wrap him in her arms. She felt a vague disappointment, the same as if the hammer of her rifle had snapped through long use. It was a good rifle, but if the hammer broke, she would make do without it. That was all.

"Kate come from Taos to find you." Israel jabbed his unlit pipe at Colter, who blinked at Israel and shifted his gaze a moment to Kathleen and then back to Israel. Colter ran a hand through his wet hair and then bent to pick up his moccasins. "She's more than two months on the trail up here. Come all that way just to see you." Colter sat on his butt and pulled on a moccasin. "Jim, you plumb forget all the manners your mamma learnt you?" Colter stared up at Israel. "Ain't you even going to say 'Howdy'?"

Colter looked at Kathleen but quickly dropped his eyes. He pulled on his other moccasin. Then he stood up and regarded Israel and Kathleen.

"Israel, you got some coffee beans? I'm a mite short, and I'd be obliged if you could spare some."

But it was Kathleen who answered, "Yeah, I got some in my gear for trade."

Colter had a pack horse tucked in the trees behind the beaver pond. He stowed his mallet and wooden trap vises on it and nodded toward the northern mountains.

"I got a cabin at the far end of the valley. There's a fire going. You're welcome to go up there and rest. There's still some grass close by for your horses. I've got more traps to set down this here creek a ways, but I'll catch up to you by and by."

"Your woman won't take a shot at strangers will she?" Kathleen asked, and Colter jerked as if she had slashed him with a whip. His eyes wide and staring, he sucked air through a gaping mouth. He wiped his face with a shirtsleeve and then shook his head.

"She knows me." A smile flashed across Israel's face, and his eyes darted from Colter to Kathleen and back. Had she not known Israel better, Kathleen would have thought her and Colter's uneasy meeting had lifted Israel's black mood. But she read the signs: the murky depths in his eyes, the stiff set of his spine, the harsh, mocking chortle. The dark mood had simply twisted in a new direction, a fresh reminder of his bitter existence. "She ain't going to shoot old Israel. Might run off with me, now, if I take a notion. So Colter, don't you be too long setting them traps."

"I'll be along."

Kathleen and Israel retraced their steps to their horses, but by the time they mounted, the strengthening winds out of the north tore at their hats and numbed their fingers.

"We'll have a foot of snow before morning," Israel shouted, and whipping off his hat and holding it out like a politician to a crowd, he roared at the mountains. "A foot of snow and no place else for us to go. Yes, sir, we going all share that little cabin together. Men, women, horses, and a mule, all snug and warm like sow bugs in a new turd."

Kathleen rode with her head down to shield her watering eyes from slashing wind and debris. Sleet stung the back of her neck. Banshee shied at every twist of the wind, mouthing the bit and jerking, but the mule plodded along with its long ears folded back and eyes masked by its thick lashes. The cold increased with every fresh gust of wind that scraped exposed skin. They edged forward along the bank of the Whiterocks until Israel whistled and pointed at a small dark-brown cabin set back among fir and pine.

"We are going to have to take the animals inside the cabin," Kathleen shouted at Israel. "Or they will freeze to death in no time."

Israel nodded his head. "Colter best give up trapping and get along quick."

"He knows how to take care of himself." Kathleen swung off Banshee and led both of her animals toward the cabin. "He will be along in his own good time."

"For a woman who spends two long months tracking him down, you don't act all that happy to see him." Israel dismounted and dragged his own horses after Kathleen.

"I never said he made me happy."

Kathleen pulled the latch string on the cabin door, shoved it open with her shoulder and, setting her feet against her reluctant animals, strained backwards pulling them across the threshold.

Hard on her heels, Israel led his two mounts through the cabin door, crowding against Kathleen and her mounts among the tight confines of the cabin. In the stone fireplace set into the far wall, the flames were low, and the moist reek of horses, drying beaver pelts, urine, and a woman in labor overwhelmed Kathleen. She gasped and blew air through her open mouth trying to clear her smarting eyes and nose. But the stench, the same as in her dreams of the buffalo calf woman, mounted, so she blinked until her eyes settled enough for her to look around.

The interior of the cabin was a narrow box no more than twenty-four feet by twenty-four feet, but fortunately, its ceiling was a rather high, sharply angled, pine thatch roof. Wooden drying hoops, most empty but a few with beaver pelts stretched tight, dangled from rafter poles. Traps, food stuffs, and odds and ends of gear were stowed against the right-hand wall. Over against the far left-hand corner, beside a pallet of furs and blankets, knelt an Indian girl with one hand against the wall. Her head was bowed, and long, unbound black hair dangled almost to the dirt floor, hiding her face. She looked to be no taller than four and a half feet.

"Israel, shut the door." Kathleen dropped the reins to her animals and in two steps crouched beside the girl. Pulling off her mittens, Kathleen tilted the girl's head up and put a palm to her forehead—clammy and chill. Her eyes were nearly closed, and her breath heaved through her tiny mouth. Spittle clung to the corners of her mouth, and the girl let out a low moan. "I said shut the door, damn it!"

"All right, all right. Let me get there. Maybe you missed it, but it's a mighty tight fit in here. Hoss, get! Go on, move your stubborn self." The horses and mule made grudging way for Israel, sidling right and left and jamming against each other. Banshee bumped against Kathleen, who shoved him away. Israel slammed the door shut. "There. Snug and warm. But I don't see how Colter and his horse going to fit in here, too. Guess we'll make room."

Kathleen shot Israel an angry look. Did he not see this poor young girl? Why must he prattle so? Israel glanced around the cabin.

"Colter's sure handy with an axe and a saw." Taking out his pipe, Israel eased through the animals toward the fire. "Most trappers make do with a lean-to or cabin half this size. But he always builds a big cabin with lots of room for his plews. Knocks it out in no time."

"He gets it from his father." Kathleen soaked a corner of a trade blanket in a gourd full of water beside the pallet and mopped the girl's face. Her eyelids fluttered open, and black pain-filled eyes stared at Kathleen.

"Huh?" Israel lit his pipe from the fire and turned toward Kathleen. "Well, I guess it's natural you know more about him. He's mighty close mouthed around me. I kind of like that. Gives me more room, so to speak. His daddy a carpenter?"

"An undertaker. Now shut up!" This was the woman giving birth in Kathleen's dreams. But this woman was hardly more than a girl: was a girl, actually. Perhaps, that was why in the dreams the cries of the woman and the child had become as one. She was, Kathleen admitted, a pretty little thing. The kind of woman a man takes in his hands and tosses in the air to listen to her squeal. To watch shining black hair bounce and dark eyes light up. To catch her and hug against his cheek smooth, unblemished skin, softer than a newborn beaver pup. Plant kisses on slender features and fine bones. And God forgive the poor dumb bastard, a man would have no idea that those small bones were too frail and slender for his seed, no idea at all.

"That wind's kicking up something bad." With his pipe lit, Israel had worked his way near the door that banged and shuddered against its sill. Indeed, the whole cabin creaked at each new gust of howling wind. "We look to be all right in here. Colter's got her chinked up good. But he's got to be struggling outside, what with his horse and traps and all. You reckon I ought to go give him a hand?"

"Yes. Go. Please."

"Well, if you think it's all right?"

"Israel, get!"

With a look of relief, Israel forced open the door and slammed it shut on Kathleen and the girl. He and Colter are both, Kathleen thought, at a loss what to do about this girl. What was happening to her was a mystery to them, something inconceivable. Oh, they knew it happened. Probably had seen dozens of animals give birth, maybe even a woman or two. But they could not conceive of what was happening within this girl's body. How something could grow inside you, the changes it caused in your body, the sensations, the feelings, and the pains—the sense that something was in you and yet not you and yet a part of you. No, they could not conceive, and so they could never conceive it. It was woman's mystery, beyond their ken, and they were uneasy in its presence.

Overwhelmed, Colter had gone to tend his traps, something he knew and understood, like a knife slash across the forearm or windage for a shot at a fleeing deer. Israel had turned gabby, the way women often did when menfolk oiled their weapons for war. Something of immense importance was happening, and he felt he should do something, try to be a part of it somehow, a help, but he had no idea what, so he gabbed, piling words on words at a time when words were of little use—when a cool head and action were needed.

Staring into the pain-filled eyes of this young girl-woman, Kathleen felt as if the long trail of her life had curved like a great hoop and brought her back to her beginning. Once again, she was in the room filled with odors of birth. There was the same clammy feel of flesh and stifling moist air. The same cries of pain. The same clawing terror churned her stomach, threatening to send her running from the room shaking and weeping.

But Kathleen was not that young girl any longer. She was the grown woman who held the hand of the young girl living through this pain and terror. She felt the presence of the Buffalo Woman of her dreams fill the cabin and felt that strange and implacable summons. There was a purpose for Kathleen O'Dwyer, the grown woman, here.

On the dirt floor, beside the pallet was a dark, wet splotch. Kathleen wiped two fingers across this splotch and sniffed her fingers. Yes, the girl's water had broken, so Kathleen pulled up the girl's buckskin dress to see how far along she was—not far, maybe a couple of hours at most. Obviously, this was the girl's first pregnancy. The bones of her small hips, the flesh and sinews of her birth canal, all were tight and firm with youth. Like the action of a new rifle, they were stiff and balky.

The girl had known enough to kneel, but Kathleen doubted the girl knew much more about birthing. She did not even have a leather strap to bite down on when the pains came, so this was her first, and even if all went without problem, there were many, many hours of pain ahead. But problems were here. Of that, Kathleen was certain. There should be fluid, but no more than a pink trace of blood this soon, yet a thin red stream trickled down one of the girl's thighs. Kathleen let the dress fall.

She did not even know the girl's name. She wanted to cradle this girl against her bosom and croon whatever the name was softly in her ear, tell her everything would be all right, feel her breathing ease and her body relax. Such a small girl. Stolen, Israel had said, from her people when she was a young child and bartered from tribe to tribe. Growing up a slave among strangers, a beast of burden like their dogs, had she ever had time to learn even one of the strange and harsh tongues of her owners?

But there was no time for comfort now. Get her up, Kathleen. The baby might be out of position. Make the girl walk. Let gravity and motion help bring on her contractions.

Getting a firm grip on the girl's left hand, Kathleen hooked her right arm under the girl's left armpit and heaved. The girl cried out, but light as she was, Kathleen had no trouble pulling her to her feet and holding her there, though she tried to sink back to the pallet.

"Walk!" Kathleen dragged the girl a step or two, ignoring agonized wailing. Kathleen placed her right leg behind the girl's left leg and lifted it in a step, then another and another. "Walk!" Clinging to Kathleen and moaning, the girl shuffled along as Kathleen led her around and around the pallet, bumping against the wall on one side and anxious horses on the other. They walked and walked, halting only when a contraction seized the girl, and then walked some more. Sometimes, she leaned her head against Kathleen's right arm, and sometimes, she trudged with head bowed, but Kathleen kept her walking. The air in the room was hot and rank with horse sweat and as an hour passed, horse droppings. Still, Kathleen walked the girl around and around the pallet. A scattered trail of red droplets sprinkled the floor. *Think, Kathleen, think.*

The door banged open, and Israel helped Colter through the doorway and let him slump, shivering, against one wall while Israel stepped outside. A moment later, he came back to the doorway, leading Colter's pack horse.

"Stop!" Kathleen glared at Israel. "Do not bring that animal in here. There is no room."

"But it'll freeze out here in this wind."

"I do not give a damn. We haven't any room." Kathleen helped the girl sit down on the pallet. Stupid, thick-headed men. Barely room in here as it was, and they propose to crowd another horse in here so it can stomp on this girl. Oh yes, there's a plan for you. Hem the girl in so she has to drop the baby in a pile of horse dung. "Keep it out, I say. And get these other beasts out of here, too. We need room."

"But Kate, they'll freeze."

"Then they freeze."

"It'll be all right, Israel." Face still grey with cold, Colter leaned his head back. "I got a lean-to out back for my horse. Built it for two animals, but a bear got the other one about a month ago. We can squeeze three or four of these animals in there. They'll be out of the wind. Should be fine."

"Well, all right." Israel pushed the horse backwards. "Out back you say?"

"Yeah. Just follow the wall. You'll find it." Colter let out a grunt and stood up. "I'll be along directly. Just need a minute to warm my hands by the fire."

Israel shoved the horse through the doorway and disappeared into the howling storm. Snow swirled through the open door with every blast of freezing wind. Colter eased toward the fireplace.

"James, close that door, for God's sake."

"Yes ma'am." He turned and shut the door. Then he crossed the room, squatted on his heels and held out his hands to the fire.

"Aren't you going to ask how she is?"

He glanced at Kathleen a moment and then stared into the fire, but Kathleen had seen the look in his eyes—the determined effort to shut out the girl and Kathleen, to barricade himself behind a wall of silent manhood. He was scared, flat scared—down deep in the gut scared of what he had set in motion without thinking. On the verge of her womanhood, this girl had come to him in a trade. He had been gentle with her, of that

206

Kathleen was certain. Colter was hard, drawn into himself, but not cruel. Probably, his was the first kindness the girl had known in years of learning that the only way to live was to give in. A soft word from him, a shy smile from her, no, it would not have taken much. Even if she had wanted to say no—and why would she?—life had taught her never to refuse. And so the way men do, he had taken her and gone on that way without thinking beyond this soft, warm pleasure in his cold, hard life. Then her belly had swollen, and he had to consider what he had done. Thinking about it had given rise to the fear, but if he acknowledged that fear, it would have a claim on him. So he treated it as he had learned to treat all fear. He refused to let it or anything that caused it touch him.

"Well then." Kathleen held the gourd to the girl's lips and let her have just a sip of water. "At least tell me her name."

"Don't know her name." Colter looked Kathleen full in the face. In his eyes, all the grim hardness was set in place, but she looked for and found the edgy wariness she had once mistaken for strength. "We, Israel and me . . . I just call her 'girl.' She answers to it well enough. I reckoned it would do." His eyes dropped for a moment. Then he looked at Kathleen. "I best give Israel a hand with these horses. Anything else you want us to do?"

Kathleen bit back the urge to tell him to go to hell. Yes, she saw that in many ways he, like Israel, was already there, but she had no time for Colter and his self-made miseries. Nor any time to wonder how that nothingness inside herself had given way to an onslaught of emotion all centered on this girl and the child she carried.

"Yes," she said, "after you are done with the horses, get a kettle boiling on the hearth. I need water—clean water. And plenty of it. Some clean rags if you have them and a scrap of leather for her to bite down on. Well? What are you standing there looking as if you were carrying the weight of the world for? It isn't you giving birth here. Go on. And make sure you close the damn door on your way out!"

CHAPTER 21

After Colter took Israel's horses to the shed, Kathleen got the girl on her feet and walking again. Her contractions were more frequent . . . but what to call her? Girl would not do. Kathleen had always liked the name Rachel, so she called the girl that over and over, getting her used to it as she had taught Banshee to recognize his name. After awhile, whenever Kathleen said *Rachel*, the girl looked at her. Once she smiled, a scared forced smile, but a smile.

Yes, she smiled, this poor little girl with a huge swollen belly that made her stick arms and legs all the more childlike. A Lakota girl born onto the Great Plains, a world of rolling grasslands from horizon to horizon. There she should have grown to womanhood with a mother, aunts, and sisters to care for her, show her the ways of a woman, guide her through the changes in her body, sing at her wedding and midwife her through her children—all the mysteries that Buffalo Calf Woman had taught Lakota women long, long ago. That had been denied this girl, and she was here fighting to give birth among strangers in these strange, dark, and terrible mountains so far from level green plains.

Kathleen, also, had crossed that ocean of grass and seen its herds of buffalo. Like this girl, Kathleen's life had changed forever on those plains. And now, Kathleen, a woman, was here with this girl, and Buffalo Calf Woman, the spirit woman of Kathleen's dreams, wanted, demanded that Kathleen help this lost Lakota girl through the greatest mystery a woman ever faced. Kathleen had never heard anyone tell the tale of Buffalo Calf Woman, but she knew it all the same and did not question how. Arm supporting the girl's frail shoulders, Kathleen hugged her a moment.

Stamping and swearing, Israel came out of the cold, followed by Colter. Kathleen shot them a look, and Israel quieted. The two men warmed themselves by the fire for a little while. Israel dug out his pipe and sat down next to the fire to smoke. Colter filled a kettle with water and set it on a flat stone in the fire. Then he found some rags and a piece of leather and brought them to Kathleen.

"She needs some ice to suck on," Kathleen said, "in a cup."

Pushing past Banshee and the mule, Colter went to the gear by the far wall. He took a tin cup off its peg and crossing the room, pushed open the door and went outside. In a few minutes, he came back inside with the cup stuffed with icicles and handed it to Kathleen. As soon as she took the cup, he retreated to the fireplace beside Israel. The two men sat there in silence, trading the pipe back and forth, and watching.

Kathleen let Rachel sit on the pallet—hang the bloodstains! If Colter did not like them, let him scrub them off, and if that was too much for him, let him shoot another buffalo for its hide—and held the cup to her lips. Soon, the kettle whistled, and Kathleen told Colter to pour the water in a pan, soak the rags, and when the water had cooled enough to handle the rags, to bring her one. She had Rachel lie down and, when Colter brought a warm rag from the pan, cleaned Rachel's belly and thighs, but the damned blood still oozed big, slow drops. Rachel's eyes were closed, but she did not sleep, for her breathing was ragged and gasping. The muscles in her calves and thighs were tense and straining. Her fists were clenched against her breasts.

"Rachel." The girl's eyes fluttered open and focused on Kathleen. "You have got to stop fighting. You must breathe right. The baby cannot come with you all tensed against the pain. You must breathe." Kathleen opened her mouth and panted. "Come on now, breathe." Kathleen panted again, but Rachel's eyes closed tight, and she grunted in pain through gritted teeth. Then Rachel gasped and whimpered low in her throat, a soft, bleating wail.

You cannot let her close in on herself, Kathleen. You must make her concentrate on letting the baby come, helping her contractions work the infant down the birth canal. She does not know how. You must teach her. You are a teacher. You have seen this often enough to know the lesson. If you cannot teach her, you will lose her and the baby.

"Up, up, Rachel." Kathleen dragged the girl, screaming and writhing, to her feet, but Kathleen held her up and made her walk again. As they walked, Kathleen called the name Rachel over and over again. Each time she said the name, she panted. Rachel cried and moaned, but after a while, she opened her mouth and panted. Kathleen patted her hair and nodded, telling her what a fine, brave girl she was. Then Kathleen panted, and again, Rachel mimicked her. They walked round and round the room, breathing in and out rapidly, while the men tended the fire, smoked their pipe, and with their hardest, most determined faces of flint, eyed the two women.

With wind howling outside, the cabin grew dark with night. The firelight dimly lit fretful, stamping Banshee, the long-eared placid mule, and the piles of trapping gear scattered along the walls. Every half hour or so, as best she could guess the passing of time, Kathleen let Rachel kneel on the pallet by the wall and sip a little bit of water while Kathleen checked the widening birth canal with her hand, for it was too dark to see. Each time, her hand came away wet with dark, reeking blood. But probe as she might with her fingertips, she could not touch the baby's head. Something was holding up its passage. A breech baby? God, forbid. Maybe, it was trying to come out feet first, but that was not likely. Ah, please be just a big headed child that with enough pushing would work its way out. Kathleen wiped her hand clean on her pant leg.

"You, James Colter, and you, Israel, you two aim to sit there smoking that damn pipe until she bleeds to death?" Kathleen barked. "Get over here and lend a hand. We must help the baby come." Colter exchanged a look with Israel. "I said get over here." Colter shrugged and climbed to his feet. Then Israel knocked his pipe against the hearth and stood up, also, but they came no closer. "Get over here, or I swear to God I will shoot you both."

"She'll sure enough do it." Israel nodded at Colter. The two men shuffled across the dirt floor and stood in front of the two kneeling women.

"I want to get her squatting on the balls of her feet," Kathleen said. "Each of you take a hold of one of her hands and help her balance."

"Why don't you just let her alone?" Colter said. Not angry, his tone was a forced offhand indifference, trying none too well to hide his fear. "Injun women always go off by themselves to have their children."

"Well now, Jim, that ain't exactly right." Israel slapped his balled right fist with the palm of his left hand. "Some do, but most go off, like the Osages, with a bunch of the tribe's womenfolk, mostly family, but no menfolk allowed. They can take care of themselves. They don't—"

"Shut up, both of you." Kathleen seized Rachel's left wrist and held it out to Colter. "Now take hold of her." Colter's hand engulfed Rachel's, covering all but the tips of her tiny fingers. Israel swore and took hold of the girl's other hand. "She is pretty weak," Kathleen said. "Grab her under the armpit with your other hand. Do not let her topple over."

Rachel's screams blended into one long, keening wail that filled the room and made Banshee neigh and butt his shoulder against the mule. But from behind the girl, Kathleen helped Rachel to squat on her haunches, and then moving quickly around in front of the girl and kneeling, Kathleen forced Rachel's knees to spread wide, ignoring her renewed gush of screaming.

"Breathe!" Kathleen panted in Rachel's face, but the girl kept on screaming and wailing. "Breathe!" Another pant had no more effect on Rachel than the first, so Kathleen slapped her hard across the cheek, seized the girl's face with her hands and blew air into Rachel's eyes. "Breathe!" Rachel opened her mouth but then gritted her teeth and cried out. "Breathe!" She blew out a ragged pant, wailed, and panted again. Whenever Rachel stopped the rapid inhaling and exhaling, Kathleen shook the girl's head.

"It's going to kill her." Israel's eyes were filled with that dark mood. His tone had a mocking certainty, as if he were reading a newspaper account of some lethal comic folly. Colter's eyes were blank, as if his consciousness had retreated into some buried recess blind to what was happening because of him.

Her hand coated in blood, Kathleen reached her fingers into Rachel, feeling for the baby's head, but her fingertips encountered a row of tiny round knobs. She traced up the knobs—fingers! They were the baby's tiny fingers—to their hand wedged hard against a side of the baby's skull. So this was the problem. Kathleen thought a moment. Should she try to force the baby back into the womb and hope the arm settled in its proper place? How much damage would she do to Rachel if she tried that? She did not know. She had only helped her aunts to midwife her mother—boiled the rags, wiped her mother's face and legs, and held her mother's hand tight when her aunts said so. Her aunts, grown women, had known how to deal with a problem birth, and only later told Kathleen whether they had turned the child or not, but they never had the time to explain all they had done to Kathleen. She would learn in due time, they had said.

A torrent of blood washed her hand. She had to get the baby out now.

"Do you have any grease or cooking oil?" she asked Colter. With that same blind look, he stared at her, so she pinched his leg. "Grease, bear grease! Do you have any? Lard, lard will do. James? James?"

Colter nodded his head. "Got some bear grease."

"Get it."

While Colter rummaged through his things for grease, Kathleen wiped Rachel's belly and loins with another rag. With her head sunk on her chest, the girl was barely conscious, hanging from Israel's grasp and moaning. Kathleen took the glob of brown grease from Colter and swabbed the opening of Rachel's birth canal.

"Is she going to live?" Colter asked. In his eyes, raw guilt had cracked the wall of denial. Kathleen had seen that pain once before in his eyes when he had told her how he had burned the house around his dead sisters and his living father. She wondered if he had the courage to face his guilt this time, or would he repair the walls of callous manhood and retreat behind them. His legs trembled, but he took hold of Rachel's hand again.

"You look a mite peaked there, Jim boy." Israel taunted Colter with a toothy grin, but his eyes shone with bitter certainty that nothing could touch him ever again. His was the mockery of the sick and dying for the living, but Kathleen had no time to pity him or Colter.

"Hold her arms up," Kathleen said, but when the two men

obeyed, Rachel screamed and twisted. "Higher! We have to straighten her spine." Kathleen used her own legs to keep Rachel's knees spread wide. The screaming became one long wail, so Kathleen shoved the strip of leather between the girl's teeth. "Hold her steady. Do not let her sag. We have to keep the passage straight."

Blood coated Kathleen's cupped hands, but after several minutes, the little fingertips showed, then hand and head, and with a rush and smacking sound, the rest of the baby, slippery with warm, reddish-purple goo and a white, cheesy slime—a girl. The umbilical cord was wrapped around the baby's neck. Only the arm pinned by the cord against the little head had prevented its strangling. Kathleen unwound the cord, and the baby let out its own loud wail.

Colter and Israel let Rachel's arms down, and Colter put a hand behind her head to ease her down.

"No!" Kathleen wiped the baby with a clean rag. "Keep her up until the afterbirth comes." The two men looked at each other. Kathleen laid the baby on the pallet. "It won't hurt her. She will barely feel it, but it has to come." Then Colter swore and tugged on Rachel's arm. Laughing at Colter, Israel raised Rachel's other arm. While the two men held the sagging girl between them, Kathleen tied off the umbilical cord with strips of torn cloth, one two inches from the baby's navel and the other six inches higher. Then with her skinning knife, Kathleen twice cut the cord between the two strips of cloth.

At a gushing, squishy sound, Kathleen looked up. The placenta formed a lumpy, flowing puddle on the ground. The two men stared wide eyed at the dark, shiny mass and then looked at Kathleen, but then a dark, thick torrent of blood spilled out of the girl, washed across the afterbirth, and streamed toward Kathleen.

"Lay her down! Lay her down!" Still holding the girl's hand,

Colter sat down behind the girl with his legs spread and cradled the girl's head in the crook of his left arm. Kathleen snatched a wad of rags and swabbed Rachel's crotch and thighs, but blood flooded out of her. Rachel's eyes were closed, and her skin was the dull brown of an old worn penny. Kathleen reached out her hand and with the back of her fingers stroked Rachel's cheek. The girl's eyes opened. She stared a moment at Kathleen and then looked past her, searching. Kathleen turned, picked up the baby, and laid her across Rachel's bosom. With a shaky hand, Rachel explored the fingers of one of the baby's hands. Kathleen slipped her knife under the collar of Rachel's buckskin dress, cut a flap to expose her breast, and helped the baby's mouth find Rachel's nipple. Then with the baby clinging to her breast, Rachel looked at Kathleen while life drained from her eyes.

When the baby finished suckling, Kathleen took her up and bundling her in clean rags and a fur pelt, sat down cross legged near Banshee and patted the infant to sleep on her shoulder. Israel sidled over to the fire and relit his pipe. Sliding Rachel off his lap, Colter straightened her corpse on the pallet with her arms folded on her bosom. Then he stood up, walked to Israel, and with his back to Rachel's corpse, held out his hand.

"I told you it was going to kill her." Israel handed the pipe to Colter, who nodded and took a long pull on the pipe stem. Then breathing out the smoke through his nose, he gave the pipe back to Israel and squatted on his heels in front of the fireplace. After a couple of meditative puffs, Israel glanced at the corpse. "Reckon we'll have to bury her now."

Colter stared at the flames. "I reckon so."

Israel cocked his head to one side. "Sounds like the storm's dying. Light's showing round the doorway. Must be dawn."

"Yeah." Colter rubbed his eyes with his fingers. "Daylight comes early up this high. Got a heap to do today. Finish that string of traps I started yesterday. Maybe get started on another up a creek at the head of the valley—if there's time. I best get started."

No, Kathleen decided, she would not weep while these two men with their narcissistic rituals of stoicism and denial shrugged off what Rachel had done. She wished Rachel's women kin were here to share her grief. Oh, then they would surely raise a proper howl to mark their sister's sacrifice, honor her courage, bid her farewell. Still, Kathleen had Rachel's baby, and when they were rid of the men's presence, she would share her tears with the daughter.

"I'll give you a hand." Israel knocked ashes out of his pipe into the fire.

"I'd be obliged to you." Colter stood up, stretched his arms and rolled his head in a slow circle. The two men turned and strode to the corpse. Each bent to seize an ankle.

"How do the Lakota dispose of their dead?" Kathleen asked. "Do they bury them, as we do?" Letting go of Rachel's legs, the two men straightened up, eyeing each other before looking at Kathleen.

"Nah," Israel said, "they fix up a platform and let the buzzards pick their bones clean."

"Then that is what you will do."

"All right, Kate." Israel and then Colter once again bent to take hold of Rachel's corpse.

"And leave her be until you have built the platform! Now, get the hell out of here."

CHAPTER 22

So the men went to build a burial platform, and Kathleen washed Rachel's corpse and bound her dark hair in two long braids. Then while Kathleen waited for the men's return, she mended the tear in Rachel's buckskin dress. The baby would wake soon and need sustenance, so she mixed honey into one of her water skins, rolled a square of thin leather into a funnel, and secured this rough nipple to the water bag with a strip of cloth. Kathleen intended to nurse the baby, but it would take two or three days of the baby's suckling to stimulate her own milk production. The honey-water would have to do until then. Yet the child would eventually starve if Kathleen did not produce milk—that she could not allow. What she needed was a wet nurse.

So Kathleen would go and find one, but would Colter come with her?

The men returned about midmorning. At Kathleen's insistence, the men wrapped Rachel's corpse in the buffalo robe before hoisting the body onto the mule. Besides the baby and her clothes, the bloody robe was all the girl owned—little enough to carry with her. In order to ride to the burial platform, Kathleen had to strap her rifle across her back so she could hold the baby in the crook of her left arm. The Hawken rode awkwardly and, in a pinch, would prove difficult to bring to bear on a target. To free her hands to ride and shoot, Kathleen meant to craft a back cradle like ones she had seen Indian women use.

The platform stood on a treeless knoll half a mile from the cabin. From here, Kathleen could see from the lake at the head of the valley to the valley's foot where foaming water marked the sudden drop of the Whiterocks down the mountainside. The men had cut lodge pole pines for uprights and cross staves and lashed them together with green willow branches.

"It's damn near twelve foot high," Israel said. "A panther might climb it, but it ought to keep off bears and coyotes."

"She will have a grand view." Kathleen smiled. "You chose well."

"I just wanted to get her far enough from the cabin to hide the stink." Israel's voice was filled with a man's worked-at mocking humor. "Colter done picked this spot."

Kathleen looked at Colter, and he met her gaze with eyes that were closed and distant, as if he were already scouting some far ridgeline half a continent away.

"Let's get her up there and be done with it," he said and dismounted, but when he shinnied up one of the uprights with a rope and hauled the corpse on top of the platform, he carefully unwrapped and arranged the body and then asked Kathleen and Israel to throw him fresh-cut pine boughs to lay across Rachel. Finished, he jumped down and stood to one side while Kathleen said a brief farewell prayer. Then they remounted their horses.

"Well, she can rot in peace now." Israel chuckled and thumped his thigh with his fist. Eyes full of pain and rage, Colter stared at Israel until the other man quieted. Then Colter kicked the ribs of his horse and cantered toward the cabin.

"Losing that girl's took the sand out of him," Israel said and grinned at Kathleen. "It'll do that to a man, but he'll get over it."

"Did you?" Kathleen kicked Banshee into a fast walk, leaving

Israel to his cursing and the mule.

When she arrived at the cabin, Colter was already busy load-ing trapping gear onto Israel's pack horse, but Kathleen meant to give him no peace. Although most of its snow had blown away, last night's storm heralded winter's arrival. The next storm might well bury the mountain passes under several feet of snow. She had to take the baby and search for a friendly Ute or Ouray village where she could barter for winter shelter and a wet nurse, and she had to know whether James Colter would go with her. Like as not, all of his thoughts, the way men often do, centered on his loss. There was a woman present to care for the child, so he had time to deal with his grief. But the child was his daughter, and Kathleen was not about to grant him a week, a day, or an hour to get over the death of the mother.

She must have his answer now while his blood was hot with guilt and pain. If she gave him time, he would retreat into cold man-made bulwarks of stoic endurance. She must not give him time to think, to reason out what was best for him, for her, for the child, or he would find that place where men mistook numb-ness for clarity, for what man ever thought himself worthy to be a husband and father? No, he must make this decision, yea or nay, filled with emotion, for only that ever truly bound a man to anything—the promise given from the depths of his heart, the oath to rise above the man that he was and be more than that, even at the cost of his life.

"You need to leave those traps to Israel." Kathleen swung down from her horse, with the baby waving her arms and cry-ing to be fed. "We have naught for your child but honey water. She needs milk, and there's none to be had in this valley."

He finished tying down a string of traps and then stood with one hand resting on the horse's load. He looked straight at her, and his eyes were bleak with despair. He was a good man damned, so he believed, by the long-past horror that a fever-ridden boy had wrought. Then he looked northward to the mountains, and his eyes filled with their distant promise of escape.

"I was kind of hoping you would look after the baby," he said. "I know I got no call to expect anything of you, but I was hoping all the same, for its sake."

"She's a girl, James, your daughter."

"I know," he said and looked again at Kathleen holding the crying infant. "But I know, too, that I ain't fit to be her father, like I knew I wasn't fit to be your husband."

"James, this girl is crying for milk." Kathleen shifted the baby to a shoulder and patted her back, but the cries only became more insistent. "I have no time to listen to you beg off your responsibilities with noble sounding excuses. Now, I'm going in the cabin to feed your daughter and put her to sleep. Then I am going to load my things and your daughter on Banshee and my mule and go searching for a band of Utes or Ourays where I can find a wet nurse for your daughter. You are fit enough to ride a horse. You make up your mind whether you're coming with us or no."

Then Kathleen went inside the cabin to feed the baby.

While the baby fed, Kathleen heard Israel come up with the mule. He said something to Colter and laughed, but if Colter answered, she did not hear it. After a few minutes, Israel came inside the cabin and sat down beside the fireplace. By then, the baby had finished with the sweetened water, so Kathleen rocked her to sleep and then laid her down on a pile of furs.

"What you going to call her?" Israel jabbed his pipe stem at the baby.

"That's for Colter to decide, if he so chooses." Kathleen collected her many bags of supplies on top of her sheet of canvas.

"You ain't leaving her with him?"

"No, I'm not leaving her—ever." There, she had said what she had felt the moment life had died in Rachel's eyes. Without question, the child was entrusted to her, and without question, she loved the child with all the fierce, ruthless love of a mother.

"Well, that's good." Israel fetched his tobacco pouch off his belt and loosened the drawstring. "Because Colter's a hell've a man, but he ain't much for settling down with no family. No true mountain man is. Got too much skedaddle in him. Likes to roam the mountains and the plains. See what's doing over the next ridge. Be free."

The baby stirred and cried out.

"Israel, see the good of all your prattle—you have waked the baby." Kathleen went over, picked up the infant, and settled her on a shoulder. Humming softly, she went outside, closing the door behind her. Israel's pack horse had drifted away from the cabin to crop sprigs of brown grass. Facing away from the cabin, Colter sat with his back against a fir tree and his forearms resting on bent knees. As Kathleen neared, he turned, looked at her, and then got to his feet.

"James, we are your last hope. But you are not ours. You are a good man, and I could love you again, and if you stay, this child will love you. But I do not know if you are capable of love any more. Maybe that aching nothingness has been inside you so long it has sucked you dry of love and hate, joy and heartache—of caring for anything. I know for a while it had a strong hold on me, but I fought it. It could come again, I know, but this child will help me fight it. She would help you, too, and so would I."

Colter looked at Kathleen a moment longer, but then his eyes shifted their restless gaze to the far mountains, so tall and sharp edged against the blue sky.

"Maybe," Kathleen said, "fight is not in you any longer. Maybe, you are like so many other men who have come west to wander the wilderness. Men like Israel. Men who have turned their backs on whatever hurt them deep in their souls and then laugh at the world and bellow how nothing can hurt them anymore. Men that let aching nothingness fill them just to wall out the pain. Yes, maybe that is you, too. God knows, you have good reasons.

"So go on if you have a mind to." She reached out and shoved him toward those wild, soaring mountains. He stumbled, caught himself, and faced her—his eyes hot and blinking. "Go on. Travel this wild land alone. See all of its beauty and splendor. Take it all in. Hear the lark sing in the sagebrush. Smell the plains awash in buffalo from horizon to horizon. For all the good it will do you. Because none of it will move you. Not one bit of it will touch your soul. Not if you can walk away from me. Not if you can walk away from this child.

"Go on! You are man enough to do it. But I am not a man. I shall hold myself to a higher accounting. I shall love this child even if you go. And I shall love the otter playing with a fish in the morning sun. And the wind that sets the water dancing. For I shall be whole."

The baby twisted on her shoulder and mewed a sleepy protest. James Colter stared at his daughter until she quieted, and then he said, "I can't see that any good will come of my staying." He glanced over his shoulder at the mountains before turning to Kathleen. "But if you're fool enough to want me, I reckon I'm fool enough to stay."

"James," Kathleen answered, "show a bit more grace when a woman comes riding to your rescue."

ABOUT THE AUTHOR

Robert Temple taught writing and literature for thirty-three years at several colleges in Florida and then retired from teaching in 2016. Mike is a veteran of the U.S. Army and earned a B.S. in Journalism from the University of Florida in 1977 and an M.A. in English, Writing Emphasis from Florida State University in 1987. Additionally, in Homosassa, Florida, he and his wife, Sheila, bred registered Suri alpacas for eighteen years, then sold the herd and farm, and currently live with their three Rhodesian Ridgebacks on five acres along a trout stream in Talking Rock, Georgia.

The employees of Five Star Publishing hope you have enjoyed this book.

Our Five Star novels explore little-known chapters from America's history, stories told from unique perspectives that will entertain a broad range of readers.

Other Five Star books are available at your local library, bookstore, all major book distributors, and directly from Five Star/Gale.

Connect with Five Star Publishing

Website:
gale.com/five-star

Facebook:
facebook.com/FiveStarCengage

Twitter:
twitter.com/FiveStarCengage

Email:
FiveStar@cengage.com

For information about titles and placing orders:
(800) 223-1244
gale.orders@cengage.com

To share your comments, write to us:
Five Star Publishing
Attn: Publisher
10 Water St., Suite 310
Waterville, ME 04901